Finding Land

Finding Land

Stories of Japan

Marian Pierce

Mirror City Press
Portland, Oregon, USA

Grateful acknowledgement is made to the following publications in which seven of these stories first appeared, some in slightly different form: "Mrs. Nakamura" in *The Mississippi Review*, "A Craving for Bread" in *Puerto del Sol*, "Finding Land" in *Scribner's Best of the Fiction Workshops 1997*, "The Hazards of Golf" in *GQ* magazine, "Tokyo Pleasureland" in *Yomimono*, "Haiku" in *Hospital Drive* and "The Grocery Store Cart" in *Portland Monthly* magazine.

The epigraph is from *The Way It Is: New & Selected Poems* by William Stafford (Graywolf Press, 1998). The poem in "Mrs. Nakamura" is from *Dewdrops on a Lotus Leaf: Zen Poems of Ryokan*, translated and edited by John Stevens (Shambhala, 1993). The haiku in "A Craving for Bread" is by Issa; the haiku in "Finding Land" is by Buson, both from *The Essential Haiku*, edited and with verse translations by Robert Hass (Ecco, 1994). The haiku in "Haiku" is by Issho and is from *Japanese Death Poems*, compiled by Yoel Hoffmann (Tuttle Publishing, 1986).

Cover photograph copyright © 2018 by Sankar Raman
Author photograph copyright © 2018 by Janice Pierce
Book design by Jennifer Omner, ALL Publications
Set in Warnock Pro and Arno Pro

They want a wilderness with a map—
but how about errors that give a new start?—
or leaves that are edging into the light?—
or the many places a road can't find?

William Stafford

Contents

Mrs. Nakamura

Mrs. Nakamura liked to look in my closets. She came in without knocking and headed straight for the closet in the six mat tatami room. She pulled aside the paper sliding door as though opening the curtain to a play, and rifled through my clothes in full view of my husband Sachio and me. "Gaijin no fuku da," she exclaimed in a tone of wonder. "The clothes of a foreigner." I gave Sachio a nudge to get his attention, and tried, in vain, to put together the words for "get out of my closet" in Japanese.

My husband politely greeted our neighbor, then went back to reading his acupuncture book. There was a bell within reach. Sachio rang it every morning at the small household shrine where he prayed to his mother's spirit. I wanted to throw it at Mrs. Nakamura, but my husband had instructed me to cultivate and maintain good relations with our neighbors, of whom Mrs. Nakamura was the ringleader and chief. She wore her gray hair in a bun, and had a voice like a Kitchen Aid mixer. She spoke what my husband called "rural Japanese." She would surely understand the phrase "Dammit, get out of my closet," if only I knew how to say it. It wasn't the kind of phrase I was learning at the Asahi Japanese Language School in Shinjuku.

Mrs. Nakamura picked lint off my collars. She touched her nose to a pleat. What was she going to take this time? I tried not to think about it. I set down the bell with nary a tinkle and walked two steps into my tiny kitchen. I threw a handful of fish flakes into a pot of boiling water. I sniffed the fishy aroma and wondered if I'd be better able to tolerate Mrs. Nakamura's errant behavior if I were about to eat matzo ball soup for lunch instead of soup made from fish flakes and fermented soybeans. That morning for breakfast we had eaten rice balls belted with seaweed, salted mackerel and radish pickles. I guessed at what I bought in the grocery store because I couldn't yet read the labels. Recently, I had purchased a box of dried squid thinking it was a box of crackers. I had washed my clothes in powder that turned out to be some kind of toilet cleaner.

Mrs. Nakamura parted blouses on their hangers and stuck her head into my closet. Sachio didn't notice. He turned a page of his acupuncture book. He was always reading to me from his acupuncture books. He brewed noxious Chinese herbs in our kitchen and made me drink the resulting potions. He inserted 24-karat gold acupuncture needles alongside my nose when I was sniffling, and nightly burned cones formed of dried mugwort leaves on my feet. Besides, what did he have to worry about Mrs. Nakamura's forays? His clothes, scarce in number and neatly folded, seemed to hold no allure for Mrs. Nakamura. Mine took up most of the closet and probably smelled of Japanese toilet cleaner. I wondered if Mrs. Nakamura would report this to the neighbors.

I tried not to think about it. I gazed out the kitchen window at the view of the water heater. The telephone rang. Without thinking I picked up the receiver and said, "Hello" in English.

"Deborah?" a familiar voice said.

"Grandma?"

"You have to visit me in Cleveland," my grandmother said without any preamble. "I'm going to die in less than a year. Your mother says you don't have what to sleep on in Tokyo. Don't the Japanese sleep?"

"Of course they sleep."

Mrs. Nakamura disappeared into my closet. Sachio had yet to give me a satisfactory explanation for her behavior. I'd broached the subject diplomatically. Was it normal for Japanese to enter without knocking, and why did Mrs. Nakamura always look in my closet?

"You're her first foreign friend," Sachio had said, and then added, with some pride, "She said your eyes are a beautiful blue. She said you look like a doll."

"They're brown," I said, "and I don't." I took off my glasses. My husband stuck his face close to mine and blinked.

"Oh." He drew his head back. "Oh," he said again.

"You might have noticed. We've been married six months. She might have noticed too."

"I see your inside beauty first."

"Inner beauty."

"Yes, inner room."

"They're like my great uncle Jule's eyes. Dark pools of light. That's what my great aunt Stella used to call them."

"Dark poor what?" my husband said. There were significant gaps when he listened to me, pauses when he lost words to dark pools of unknown meanings. I had to pick and choose carefully when I spoke to him, scale down my vocabulary, avoid fancy metaphors. What it came down to was that I had to learn Japanese. I was trying to learn Japanese. I went to Japanese language school daily and sometimes to the public baths, where I practiced my language skills in the buff with naked old ladies, who added cold water to the tub when they saw me coming, and peppered me with questions. Was the water still too hot, and when was I going to get pregnant? Did I like raw egg over rice, and did I always turn bright red when I was bathing?

"Even in Poland I had a bed," my grandmother said.

"I have a bed. What time is it there?"

"It's two forty-five. You should be asleep."

There were no signs of life from within my closet. What WAS Mrs. Nakamura doing in there? Whatever she was doing, it was too quiet to hear over the clatter in Cleveland. My grandmother cooked and cleaned when upset, even at three in the morning, and had recently been threatened with eviction from her Shaker Heights apartment building for frequent nighttime vacuuming. I hoped that she wasn't vacuuming.

"You're mother says you're learning Japanese," my grandmother said. "You never learned Hebrew. Come home. Learn Hebrew. Get some decent sleep."

I jumped at the sound of the vacuum cleaner, and then realized it was the phone, crackling with static. If I was lucky, the satellite beaming messages between America and Japan was about to fall into the ocean. I didn't want to return to Cleveland, where the sky was gray from pollution. A cold wind blew off Lake Erie, and the Cuyahoga River caught fire and burned. Now every morning I took the rush hour train to the heart of Tokyo, packed in among the Japanese businessmen. They exhaled the fragrance of breakfast: rice, fish, and cigarettes. They read sports newspapers containing pictures of naked women but few of sportsmen. They never said a word.

"Grandma, are you vacuuming?" I said as soon as the crackling had subsided. "You know you're not supposed to be vacuuming at three in the morning."

"It's three oh-five. Who can vacuum? Your mother took away my Hoover and gave me a dust roller. The neighbors are sleeping like babies. You'll sleep like a baby here, too."

"I sleep fine in Tokyo."

"Without a bed? Says who?"

"I have a bed, it's just a different kind of bed. In the morning we fold it up and put it in the closet. At night we lay it down when we want to go to sleep."

"What kind of bed is that?"

"It's a futon. You've heard of futons. Lots of people in America have them."

"Phooey what? I don't know how you speak that rotten language on no food and no sleep."

"It's not a rotten language."

"You turned down your nose at Hebrew. I threw out my girdle and I'm flying to Jerusalem to visit Sam and Gertie. Before I go, I'll freeze and wrap my challah. I'll send it by first-class mail."

"Who's Sam, and what did you do with your girdle?"

"I threw it away. My bra, too. I met Sam at the Cleveland Clinic. Dr. Steinman gave me new heart pills, but what good they'll do, who can say? I may die on Sam's sofa in Jerusalem. I may die while I'm kneading this bread dough. Then you won't in your whole life eat another challah, and you'll be sorry you didn't visit me in Cleveland!"

"You're not going to die. You always say you're going to die."

"This time I have a feeling. Despite Steinman, this time I know."

"What are you doing going to Jerusalem, then? Stay home! Take care of yourself. You're eighty years old."

"Eighty-one, with a bad heart. Why should I stay home? Did you?"

I heard a thud and then nothing. "Grandma? Hello?" There was no sound of breathing. No dial tone. Only silence. I pressed the receiver to my ear and strained to hear the slap of bread dough on the kitchen counter, the slurp of Grandma drinking her Sanka and cream. "Grandma?" She'd had a heart attack. She was lying stricken in her kitchen. In addition to throwing away her undergarments, she'd neglected to take her heart medicine. She'd overexerted herself flirting at the Cleveland Clinic and cooking and baking until three in the morning. She'd keeled over baking bread dough topless.

I hung up the phone and dialed my parents. There was no answer. Where were they, and could I call 911 all the way from Tokyo? I turned off the stove. I rummaged in a desk drawer for my passport, then headed for the closet to get my suitcase. I had only gone two steps forward when the closet door slid open with its customary rumble and Mrs. Nakamura burst forth like a projectile shot out of a cannon, narrowly missing Sachio, who was still planted dead center, reading. In a white blur she flew around the room as though forty years younger, finally slowing enough to reveal that she was wearing my greatest treasure, a gossamer white nightgown with billowy sleeves and a row of red sequins stitched into the bodice (several of which modestly hid my nipples), which had been purchased in the moment of weakness that seizes every bride-to-be. Who knew whether or not Tokyo had a Victoria's Secret? Nobody in Cleveland.

"Oh," my husband said, at last taking notice of something. "She found your nightwear. I think she likes it."

I had never seen Mrs. Nakamura in anything but a housedress and an apron. Now she floated beaming around the room within the gossamer cloud of my nightgown. Sequins sparkled in the region of her belly button. The hem of my nightgown fell below her knees. I shut my eyes. I felt slightly dizzy.

"Gohan ga takemashita," the rice cooker said in a tinny voice.

"The rice is cooked," Sachio said. "Mrs. Nakamura looks pretty."

I ventured a peek at my half-naked neighbor. She appeared to be wearing nothing underneath my Victoria's Secret.

"Gohan ga takemashita," the rice cooker repeated. It would continue repeating itself, like a parrot, until someone pressed a button on its panel.

I hadn't wanted to buy a talking rice cooker. I hadn't wanted to buy the head-cooling pillow that Sachio plugged in on hot summer nights before we went to sleep. It made me shiver, which was due, my husband said, to a weak liver function and poor circulation in my extremities. He'd purchased me an electric blanket. He'd bought, and then installed, a special toilet seat which heated up to eighty-three degrees Fahrenheit when you sat on it, then squirted water of a similar temperature at your fanny when you'd finished your business. For a grand finale, it shot out blasts of hot air and dried everything. I hadn't want to purchase a special toilet seat. I didn't like getting boiled alive in the public bath while naked old ladies interrogated me with questions of a personal nature and exclaimed that I was turning scarlet, and I didn't enjoy getting stuck with acupuncture needles, even when made of precious metals. I wanted Sachio to notice me, but he no longer noticed me. Tokyo had transformed him from a romantic who recited Japanese poetry into an oriental medicine fanatic, an acupuncturist extraordinaire, and not even my Victoria's Secret could distract him. While I read Jane Austen on our double futon, clad in practically nothing but two red sequins, he studied the color-coded chart of the acupuncture meridians which folded out from the center of his textbook.

"What are you doing with my nightgown?" I asked Mrs. Nakamura when she came to a halt in front of me. She only pinched the silky-soft material of the nightgown between her fingers and said, "Utsukushii." Beautiful. She lifted the hem of the nightgown until her thighs were showing. Her hips appeared. Sequins glittered.

"What the heck is Mrs. Nakamura doing?" I said to Sachio. "Look at her. No, don't look. She's doing a striptease."

"She's playing dress-down."

"Dress-up."

"Yes, undressing. She's enjoying."

Mrs. Nakamura slid the nightgown up over her breasts. The telephone rang. Mrs. Nakamura let go of my nightgown, and the folds swirled back down around her. She picked up the receiver and said brightly into it, "Obá-san?"

"My grandmother! Is that my grandmother?"

"I think it is," Sachio said. "How funny. Nakamura-san is asking Grandma if she owns peek-a-seek nightwear. Does she?"

I snatched the telephone out of Mrs. Nakamura's hand and held the receiver to my ear. "Grandma? Are you okay?"

"Why wouldn't I be?"

"I heard you fall. What happened?"

"I didn't fall. I dropped the bread dough. Eight loaves worth. Such a sound it made. I woke up the neighbors, even old Mrs. Landau. She was mad as a hatter. I shouted into her good ear, 'Edith, how much do you sleep at eighty-five anyway?' 'I'm seventy-five,' she lied but you have to keep the peace with your neighbors, so did I say anything to her? My lips were sealed. Luckily my kitchen floor is clean enough to eat off of. With this bread in your belly, you'll sleep like Rip Van Winkle. So when are you coming to Cleveland?"

"Next week. As soon as I can get a ticket. I'm worried about you. Baking bread at all hours of the morning. Throwing away your bra. Flirting with some old guy at the Cleveland Clinic. At your age."

"We don't flirt. We talk in Yiddish. We exchange recipes."

"Your boyfriend cooks?"

"Who, Sam? He eats. His wife cooks. You wouldn't know it. Gertie's a bone with no meat on it, a stick off a tree, like you. What are they feeding you in Japan, and when did you say you were coming to Cleveland?"

"Next week."

"You can't come. Your mother is taking me to the airport the day after tomorrow. She's putting me on a plane to Israel and then going to the post office to mail you your challah. Two loaves, frozen so they'll keep."

"Why didn't you tell me you were going to Israel?"

"I told you. You're too tired to listen. You need a decent bed and sleep."

"I have a bed."

"Even a dog has its doghouse. A mouse has its mouse hole."

"I have a bed."

"A mouse hole. The floor. I know."

"Grandma, why have you been pestering me to come to Cleveland if you knew you were going to Jerusalem?"

"I didn't know you were coming next week. You've only been married six months."

"What does that have to do with anything?"

"It's too soon to leave your husband. When are you going to have a baby? I'll call you back in five minutes. I'm putting the bread in the oven."

I heard the familiar sound of my grandmother's oven door creaking on its hinges, followed by a click and the dial tone. I hung up the phone. I wasn't going to Cleveland.

"Gohan ga takemashita," the rice cooker said again. Mrs. Nakamura walked over to it and pressed the blinking red light on its panel. She lifted the lid and peered into the cooker. Let her eat some. Maybe I'd join her, because I wasn't going to Cleveland. I didn't need to go because I had just been there on my honeymoon six months ago. Nobody went to Cleveland on their honeymoon, especially not the Japanese. They went to Niagara Falls or Times Square or Disneyland. They rode to the top of the Eiffel Tower in Paris. If they were hard up for cash, they went to a hot spring resort in Izu. They certainly didn't go to Cleveland, but we had gone and I wanted to go again. I wanted my grandmother's bread, made by my grandmother, modestly attired in her brassiere and apron. I didn't want to eat bread frozen in a box and delivered by the Japanese postal service. It would probably be stale. If it made it to Japanese borders, it would be quarantined in Narita Airport by inspectors who couldn't recognize a loaf of bread when they saw it. They'd ban it as an unrecognizable foreign object. Nobody here ate bread. They ate rice made by rice cookers that talked to them rudely. They ate dried squid instead of crackers. They ate fish for breakfast.

I took out my carry-on bag and unzipped it. I opened drawers and tossed out socks and underwear. I put *Pride and Prejudice* in my carry-on bag. I folded my Smoky Bear T-shirt. *Don't Start Forest Fires.* I wanted to pack my nightgown, but how was I going to get Mrs. Nakamura to relinquish it? My wayward neighbor was now fluffing up the rice with the plastic ladle. This at least was normal behavior, even if it wasn't the normal attire for doing it in. Everyone in Japan fluffed up the rice as soon as it finished cooking. Everyone said please and thank you at the same time, and for the same reasons. Everyone always behaved as they were supposed to, except for Mrs. Nakamura.

"Are you going somewhere?" Sachio asked.

"I'm going to Cleveland."

"We were just there."

"I'm going again. Something's wrong with my grandmother. First she claimed she was dying and begged me to come to Cleveland, and then when I said I was coming, she told me she was jetting off to Jerusalem. She has heart problems. She's elderly and shouldn't be going anywhere. Why is my mother letting her?"

"Jerusalem is holy land. Maybe Grandma wants to turn inwards, like a monk. She wants to be in a holy place. This is normal, at her age."

"Normal is not throwing away your bra and flying halfway across the world to visit strangers you met at your cardiologist's office."

"She threw away what?"

"Her bra and girdle. I don't know what's gotten into her."

"A bra and girdle is not good in oriental medicine. Constriction around the chest and abdomen is inadvisory."

"Not advised."

"Yes, unwise. It compresses the internal organs."

"She's not thinking about her internal organs."

"Maybe she just wants to play dress down, like Mrs. Nakamura."

"Dress-up. I don't want her to play dress-up. I want her to stay in Cleveland so I can eat bread in her kitchen."

"You can buy bread at the Sun Merry Bakery."

"That's not bread. It's Styrofoam. Sawdust. Fluff. Cotton wool. It turns to charcoal in the toaster oven. No wonder you call it 'pan.' It's as inedible as a hunk of metal. It's not bread, and who can eat in our kitchen with nowhere to sit and that rice cooker yapping at you? I don't like having to plug in my pillow, either. What happened to plain old goose feathers?"

"You need that head-cooling pillow. You're hothead."

"It makes me shiver. I can't fall asleep when my body temperature plunges below freezing."

"This is because of weak liver function and poor circulation in your extremes."

"Extremities."

"Yes, I'll remedy this. I'll give you acupuncture. Your heat is all in your head because of too much thinking. You shouldn't think so severely. You should just enjoy and play dress-down, like Nakamura-san."

"Dress-up."

"Yes, undress. Don't be homesick. Be comfortable. This is your home here in Hibarigaoka."

"It's not my home, it's yours."

"Anywhere you are is home for me. Do you want to go to Cleveland? I'll go with you to Cleveland. I can live anywhere. I'm like Ryokan. Famous Zen monk and poet. His name is the same as a Japanese bean sweet." Sachio selected a book from his bookshelf and flipped through the pages. He recited:

> If someone asks
> My abode
> I reply:
> "The east edge of
> the Milky Way."

> Like a drifting cloud,
> bound by nothing:
> I just let go
> Giving myself up
> To the whim of the wind.

"Do you like it?"

"I'm not a cloud," I said. "I'm a human being, however dumb in this language. I can't say anything. What has gotten into Mrs. Nakamura? I can't ask her, because all I know how to say is my name is Deborah and please and thank you and excuse me."

"That's important too."

"It's not important."

"Mrs. Nakamura is just enjoying. She said she is boring until you came from America. Me too."

"But you don't take any notice of me. You just study acupuncture all the time and stick me with needles. I'm your human pincushion."

"You're nice wife. Good person. Kindly to everyone."

"Look where it's gotten me. I'm a spectacle for the neighbors. They stare at me when I'm bathing, ask me nosy questions, and rummage through my closets."

I watched Mrs. Nakamura open our kitchen cupboards, but I didn't care, because I was going to Cleveland. Sachio said, "She must be hungry.

She looks very happy in your nightwear, don't you think so?" I put my Smoky Bear T-shirt in my carry-on bag. I didn't answer my husband. Mrs. Nakamura took a rice bowl out of the cupboard and filled it with rice from the rice cooker, then set a pair of chopsticks across the top of it and came smiling towards me. The telephone rang. My grandmother. I picked up the receiver.

"Grandma, I can't talk long. I'm having a pajama party with my neighbor."

"Tabete kudasai," Mrs. Nakamura said. "Please eat." She presented the rice bowl to me and then held an imaginary cup of tea to her lips. She drank from it deeply, although, with green tea, one was only supposed to sip. She whispered "Ocha nomu?" Will you drink tea?

"We're having a pajama and tea party," I repeated to my grandmother. "My neighbor makes Japanese sweets out of mashed beans. She's inviting me over for some now. She always serves me green tea and sweets made from mashed beans."

"They're not mashed beans," Sachio said.

"Anyone with no bed would have mashed sleep," my grandmother said.

"They're not mashed beans," Sachio said. "They're azuki beans. They go very well with green tea." He had been raised on a green tea farm in Shizuoka. This made him a hit with our neighbors, each of whom we'd presented with a tin of shin-cha, or green tea made from the newest spring growth of tea leaves. Mrs. Nakamura always invited me over to drink this tea after raiding my closet. The last time she had seized my new men's jacket, a reversible creation that was red on one side and green on the other, and had plunged her hand delightedly in every pocket and then down each sleeve.

"Go ahead," my husband said. "Be neighborly. I'll talk to Grandma. Drink tea and eat sweets."

"Anyone with no bed would have mashed sleep," my grandmother repeated. "You tell your husband. Buy a bed. You need your sleep."

"Grandma, can you hold on a second? Please?" I put down the rice bowl. I covered the receiver. I said to Sachio, "Tell Mrs. Nakamura I'd be happy to eat beans if she'd stop stealing my clothes. Why does she steal my clothes? Can't she just invite me over for tea?"

"She doesn't steal. She returns. She returned your returnment jacket."

"Reversible jacket. But before she returned it, she made me eat the mashed beans."

This wasn't strictly true. She had served me a slice of Castella, the buttery pound cake introduced to the Japanese by Dutch traders, who had been confined to a small area in Kyushu because of their strange red hair, bushy beards, and religious ideas. In those days Westerners had been called—and were still sometimes called—butta kusái, "stinks of butter." Presumably whatever buttery odor I emanated was tempered by my intake of beans.

"I've figured out your modi operandus," I said to Mrs. Nakamura. "You swipe an article of clothing, and then corral me into going to your place to eat mashed beans. Go ahead. Ransack my closet. Try on my lingerie. Feed me mashed beans."

Mrs. Nakamura smiled and nodded, as I smiled and nodded when she spoke to me. She brought the cup of imaginary tea to her lips and took a gulp. She pointed to the door, and waited for me to nod that I would follow her. I nodded. How else was I going to retrieve my nightgown? I said to my grandmother, "Sachio wants to talk to you" and handed him the telephone.

"Hello, Grandma? It's Sachio. How are you?"

"I'm going to Cleveland," I said to Mrs. Nakamura in Japanese. "To America."

"Dokó e?"

"To Cleveland, that's where," I repeated. "To my inaka, my birthplace. Not to your house for tea."

Mrs. Nakamura's smile faded. Her cheeks drooped. She looked at me so sadly, I had to look away. I pretended to be looking at something nice out the window, at a cloud or a flower, though neither could be seen, only buildings and the heap of beer bottles the guy in the apartment building next door always tossed onto the tiny square of earth between our apartment building and his. We couldn't get him to stop. Mrs. Nakamura was still looking at me. I could hear the deep breath she took. "Toshi o totta na," she said. "Toshi o totta na."

"You're going to Jerusalem?" Sachio said into the telephone. "That's wonderful!"

"Toshi o totta na," Mrs. Nakamura cried out. I didn't know what it meant, but she sounded very unhappy. She walked over to the full-length mirror next to our closet and somberly inspected her reflection.

"Toshi o totta na," she repeated. A torrent of words followed. A tear rolled down her cheeks. I couldn't bear it. I tugged at my husband's sleeve.

"What's she saying? What does 'toshi o totta na' mean? She was so happy a minute ago."

"Grandma, can you hold on one second? My wife needs help talking to our neighbor."

"What's she saying?"

"Be quiet so I can listen. Oh! She says she became old lady. She says she looks like witch. No, like demon."

"She doesn't look like a witch. How can she say that? For a sixty-five year old woman she looks pretty good in that nightgown. Tell her."

"She says if you are going to America you have to take your nightwear with you. She says she will turn from princess to frog, like in a fairy tale she saw on TV. Grim fairy tale. Now she's saying she's old lady who never went anywhere in her whole life. She only stays in Tokyo."

"I thought she was born in Niigata. Doesn't she ever go there?" I looked in my closet for a handkerchief.

Sachio kept on translating. "She says Niigata is country place of Japan. Just a village. Doesn't count. She says she never went on trip, never anywhere, because her husband is a hataraki mono."

"A what?"

"Man who is working hard. All the time working hard. Six days, seven days a week. She is afraid he will die of karoshi. He never takes trip with her. Never enjoys. Life is boring until Miss America came. But now she's going."

I couldn't find a handkerchief. I dabbed at my eyes with the nearest thing I could grab, then noticed I'd used Mrs. Nakamura's housedress. I stuffed it in a corner of the closet. I balled up her apron. She was so dazzled by my nightgown she'd surely forgotten about her housedress and apron. But she no longer seemed dazzled, and I wanted her to be dazzled. I found a handkerchief and gave it to her, but she only stood holding it by one corner, weeping. Her shoulders drooped within their gossamer curtain.

"Tell her I'm not going to America forever," I said to Sachio. "Tell her."

"You said 'Amerika e kaerimasu' to Mrs. Nakamura. That means I'm returning to America. Forever. She's upsetting. Me too. I asked you before, do you want to stay in America? But you said no. You said you want to try Tokyo."

"I did. Do. I only meant that I was going to America, not staying there forever."

"But you didn't say 'Amerika e ikimasu.' You said 'Amerika e kaerimasu.'"

"That was a mistake."

"You have to speak correct Japanese."

"Tell her I'm only going for a visit."

"You tell her. I'm not your marionette. I can't do all your talking. Grandma? Sorry for waiting. I'm going to take the phone away so I can talk to you."

My husband fled into our four mat tatami room and closed the sliding door behind him. Mrs. Nakamura was still crying. I dove into my closet and took out my favorite pair of bell-bottoms, which I'd purchased in the seventies after listening to Eric Clapton croon *Bell Bottom Blues* on a friend's album. My bell-bottoms were covered with a leopard skin pattern. I wore them with shiny black shoes, though I hadn't worn them once in Tokyo. I held them out to Mrs. Nakamura. Her eyes brightened. She wiped her face with the handkerchief and reached for the bell-bottoms.

"They're yours," I said. She stroked one leg, and then the other. She lifted my Smoky Bear T-shirt out of my carry-on bag and handed it to me.

"You," she said in English. "You."

I took off my shirt. I put on Smoky instead. Mrs. Nakamura mimed putting on my bell-bottoms, and then gave them back to me. "You," she said in English. "You."

I held the bell-bottoms up to my waist. I looked at myself in the mirror. Leopard skin bell-bottoms would look odd with a Smoky Bear T-shirt, but what the heck? This wasn't Cleveland. I took off my jeans and slipped on the bell-bottoms. They felt cool and smooth and strong, like wind or water. Mrs. Nakamura stepped up beside me. We smiled like crazy at our reflections and then sailed out the door together.

A Craving for Bread

"Go to the supermarket," my husband said. "Buy something for breakfast and lunch." So I put on the pair of jeans without the holes in the knees and a plaid blouse that had looked okay in Seattle but was all wrong for Tokyo. I paused at the door and thought about changing my clothes. I ran back to my closet, hoping that something right to wear would appear in place of my yellow plastic raincoat draped on a hanger, the khaki pants just right for a hike on Mt. Rainier, my red overalls. The only Japanese I had seen in overalls were two years old.

"I have to go shopping for clothes," I said. I had said this to him every day since we had arrived in Tokyo five months ago. I didn't tell him that I got frightened when I went into the department store, where salesladies in smart blue uniforms with blue vests and white blouses stood at the entrance, wearing heels much too high for all of the subway steps they trudged up and down each day, bowing gracefully to me from the waist, their hands pressed to the fronts of their thighs, their sleek black hair swinging forward in hospitality. Their stockings never had runs in them. "Irrasháimase," they said. Welcome. Welcome, welcome, welcome. I could never run the gauntlet of welcomes, I always ended up turning back for the door. "Dōmo arigatō gozaimásu," they would call out as I exited. Thank you very much. For nothing, I hadn't bought anything, I hadn't even gotten as far as lady's gloves on the first floor. For etiquette, is what he would say. It's not for nothing. It's all for etiquette.

He drilled etiquette into me. I thought about everything before I did it, his instructions ran in my head like the language tapes I listened to at night. Itchi, ni, san, shi, gó and all the rest up to one hundred. "The Miss Manners of Tokyo," I called him.

"It's for your own good," he said in defense of his mission to teach me the finer points of behaving like a Japanese. "In Japan we have a saying that the nail that sticks up gets pounded down. I don't want you to stick out like a sore finger."

"Thumb," I corrected.

"Okay, thumb." He loved learning American idioms. Every time he learned a new one, he used it over and over again until I went mad. "Now do you remember what I was saying about slippers?"

"Don't walk out of the bathroom wearing the bathroom slippers."

"That's right. You'll stick out like a sore thumb. Japanese etiquette is a piece of cake, isn't it?" he added, and went on about slippers and other points of etiquette without missing a beat. Always step into the guest slippers that the hostess has set out for you just inside the door. If you are the hostess, don't forget to place the guest slippers on the floor. Don't wear slippers at all on tatami mats. Never ever pass food directly from your chopsticks to mine. Why? After someone's died, the family takes their cremated remains and passes the bones that are left directly from chopstick to chopstick. (It sounded weird enough to be true.) You have your own rice bowl, your own pair of chopsticks, your own bowl for miso soup and your own teacup. Everyone has their own. It's more sanitary, isn't it? Remember to say "itadakimásu" before you eat and "gotchisōsamadéshita" after. When you bring the rent to the landlady call out "ojamashimáshita" as you open the paper sliding door. What does that mean? Excuse me for being in the way. Always take a bath before you go to bed. Sit on the little plastic stool and wash yourself thoroughly with the body shampoo. Then rinse off and step into the tub. Add cold water if it's too hot for you. Japanese like their baths scalding, but we don't expect foreigners to be able to tolerate all that heat. Then there were the instructions about bedding and the direction you were supposed to lie in so as not to get nightmares, but I tried not to think of those this early in the day.

"Your clothes don't matter," he said. "You're just going to the supermarket."

Then why did our neighbor, Mrs. Nakamura, love to slide aside my closet door and look over my clothes? Why did she always murmur, "Gai-jin no fuku da," "the clothes of a foreigner," in that knowing tone? Why did she finger my fabrics and inspect my hems?

"She's a little strange," my husband said. "She's not a typical Japanese. Your clothes are fine. There's nothing wrong with them."

I didn't believe him. I tried to remember what Japanese women typically wore to the supermarket. Whatever they wore, I certainly didn't have it in my closet. I took off my blouse.

"Wow," my husband said. "Make hay while the sun shines." He sat up on his futon and grabbed my ankle. I pulled it away and kept on worrying about what to wear. Maybe the Japanese would be too busy choosing ripe peaches and looking into the eyes of fish to pay any attention to my attire. I'd trailed around the supermarket many times with my husband, trying to keep my mind on food rather than the customers' clothes. Luckily the food fascinated me, especially the things we didn't buy, cuts of whale meat at five hundred yen each, brown globs floating in liquid that I could never remember the name of, packaged sheets of seaweed that looked like green papyrus. Instead we bought thick white radishes that I said were shaped like candles and he said were shaped like Japanese women's legs. He liked my legs better. The radishes ended up cooked in miso soup or shredded with carrot to make a salad that he claimed was good for the digestion. I figured I was going to spend the rest of my life trying to master the etiquette around food and cooking, not to mention digestion, but for the moment I'd be happy if I learned how to season the soup stock, which you couldn't boil too long or the fish flakes went bitter and spoiled the taste. What did he want me to buy at the supermarket? He lay back down on his futon and pulled the quilt over his head.

"Whatever you want," he said from under the sheets. This put me into a panic. I tried to calm myself. After all, I'd backpacked around India, what were a few choices from a supermarket shelf compared to trying to get a seat on the Madras Express without a reservation, or fighting my way through a sea of elbows onto a bus in Bombay? Okay, I said, I can handle it. I put on my Grand Canyon T-shirt. It had a picture of Smoky Bear on the back. Anything with English lettering on it was wildly popular in Japan. *Don't Start Forest Fires.* Would anybody be able to read that? I squared my shoulders, stepped into my shoes, and headed out the door.

Japanese women walked with short strides and erect backs. "Itte kimasu," I remembered to say as I left, although it looked like he had gone back to sleep. That meant, "I'm going and coming back." "Itte rash shai," he called out. "Go, and welcome back."

The door closed with a resounding clang. All went silent behind it. I had a terrible craving for a slice of bread. If I asked him to buy a loaf when he went to the supermarket he said, "Bread isn't good for you, it swells up in your stomach and disturbs your chi." So much for marrying an acupuncturist. When I ate bread in our apartment he'd invariably comment on the swelling and the chi and I'd get a stomach ache and he'd say, "I told you not to eat that. Have you been drinking milk too? Milk causes mucus to form in the intestine, and eating fruit with bread is a particularly bad idea." My grandmother, who had tried for years to temper my parents' atheism by stuffing me with Jewish foods, had sent unexpected reinforcement in the form of a loaf of her challah, which she had frozen, surrounded with bubble packing, and taped up in a box. It cost her twenty dollars to ship.

"I'm drooling," said my best friend Linda, when I called her to announce the arrival of my grandmother's bread. "Did Sachio try some?"

"Are you kidding? He rapped on it with his knuckles and warned me that it would sit in my stomach for fifty years."

"How nice of him to praise her baking."

"Then he said it would wreak havoc with my chi."

"Of course. His usual line. Save me a piece."

"He glared at me so hard I couldn't eat it. I can't figure out why. Six months ago he gobbled down an American breakfast at my parent's house and asked for seconds on everything, including the buttered bagels."

"They always do that on the honeymoon," Linda said.

"The only thing he wanted that we didn't serve him was bacon. My grandmother would have had a fit."

"Why don't you eat bread outside?"

Eating on public streets was a breach of etiquette that I wasn't about to commit. In Japan you were supposed to eat behind closed doors, although it was, of course, perfectly okay to eat in a restaurant. No Japanese in their right mind would eat squid-flavored potato chips as they walked down the street. You could stand at the sweet potato seller's cart on a cold winter's day in Ueno Park and eat your sweet potato. But to walk munching down the park paths was just not the done thing.

"I know," Linda said. "Eat bread at home while he's at work."

"I can't. He'd be sure to smell it on me. He has a nose like a champion hunting dog's."

Linda's husband smoked and couldn't smell anything. If my husband didn't sniff out the bread, the butter would tip him off. Japanese called Americans "butta kusái," "smells of butter." Besides, I couldn't eat a whole loaf at once, and where would I hide the rest of it?

"How ridiculous," Linda said. "You should eat what you want. He eats rice every day, so why shouldn't you eat bread?"

I didn't want to put up with the hassle he'd give me about the consequences to my health, I told her. We all make our compromises to live here; we have to choose our fights. Why does Carol Tanaka allow her husband to go drinking every day after work when she's stuck at home with the baby? Who cares if businessmen are required to socialize, who cares if it's part of the job, does she always have to be the one to change the diapers? Then again I sometimes wished I was married to someone who came home late and didn't keep an eye on everything I did. What privacy could I have with a man who kept tabs on my chi, and noticed when my yin was out of balance with my yang?

"At least he notices something," Linda said. Her husband came home too tired to do anything but wolf down dinner, belch, compliment her on her cooking, and turn on the TV. My husband accused the TV of emitting radiation, and kept it in a corner of our eight-mat room with a cloth over it. He only unveiled it during national emergencies.

"What does he do when he comes home from work?" Linda wanted to know.

"He observes me and makes comments on what he sees. He grabs my wrist and feels my pulse. He tells me I'm going to have my period in a day. He instructs me in cooking and in etiquette."

"Golly," Linda said.

"Ohio," Mrs. Nakamura said.

"I'd shoot him," Linda said. She was from Texas, and couldn't get the Wild West out of her blood. I pictured her in her stitched cowboy boots and broad-rimmed Stetson, silver revolvers at the ready, taking aim at my husband's head. Instead I looked up to find Mrs. Nakamura standing in the hallway of our apartment building, laundry basket in hand, beaming at me above clean sheets.

"Ohio," she said again.

"Ohio," I said. That meant good morning and was easy to remember. Every day when I woke up my husband said "Ohio, Cleveland," which is my birthplace and a pretty good joke. Mrs. Nakamura put down her laundry basket. She looked ready to engage in a long chat. What an optimist. She apparently never gave up hope that I had learned more Japanese than I knew since the last time she had talked to me, twenty-four hours ago. She always started our conversations with a one-word greeting followed by a two-word question, building slowly and carrying on my part of the conversation when I got lost.

"Dokó e?" she asked. Where are you going?

My husband said that "dokó e?" was just a polite phrase, like, "How are you?" Americans asked "How are you," and Japanese asked "Where are you going," and neither required a serious answer. He had taught me a stock reply to this question, but for the moment I couldn't remember it, so I just said "Supaa," meaning supermarket, another easy word to remember. I hurried towards the door to head off further conversation. "Itte rasshai," Mrs. Nakamura said, picking up her basket. She added another smile to the one already on her face. On the street I remembered what I should have said to "Where are you going?" I was always remembering things after I needed them. Did this usually happen in foreign languages, I wondered. "Chótto soko e." I'm just going a little somewhere. But where?

A sudden picture of my husband sitting down to brunch at my parent's Formica kitchen table in Cleveland flashed into my mind. I saw the big bites carved out of his onion omelette, the syrup swimming on his buttermilk pancakes, the abandon with which he'd slapped lox on a bagel. Perhaps if I cooked him an American breakfast it would remind him of our honeymoon and he'd forget to complain about the bread. I would sizzle bacon and fry eggs and toast bread in the oven. I'd fill up my cup with good quality Hokkaido milk and top if off with a dollop of coffee. I pictured the egg yolks' gleaming golden eyes, crisp curls of bacon, and

Ravel's *Bolero* playing on our tape recorder. At the height of the music, the part where it gets louder and faster, dum da dee dum, I'd bite into my toast. A thick slice of toast made from the soft, white bleached fluff they passed off as bread in the local supermarket. Slathered with butter that dripped down my chin. No, it would never do. If I couldn't have challah, I wanted whole wheat. At least it was healthier than white bread. But where could I buy it? Surely there was somewhere to buy it. Japan was consumer heaven if you could pay the price and didn't get scared off at the door.

I would go back to our apartment and ask Mrs. Nakamura. But did she eat bread? I knew the word for bread, but what in the world was that funny word for wheat? I hummed "Boogie Woogie Bugle Boy," the song I'd learned after I knew five chords on the guitar. Then I remembered the word for wheat. Moogie. The word for bread was pan, pronounced differently than the cooking utensil, with an "ah" like a sigh in the middle. Moogie pan. Where can I buy moogie pan?

"Ikebukuro," Mrs. Nakamura said. "Ikebukuro depaato." She pinned a sheet to the line.

The dreaded Ikebukuro Department Store. But of course. They had absolutely every food known to man in the grocery section in their basement. French bread in the bakery too, according to Mrs. Nakamura. If I caught the express train I'd make it to Ikebukuro in seventeen minutes, thirty by the slower train. I curbed my impulse to run. Where's the fire, somebody might shout at me if they spied me running. Particularly if they could read the English on my shirt. Japanese women didn't run up the street unless they were chasing their children. What children, Mrs. Nakamura wanted to know. She studied my stomach for signs of growth; she often pointed to it in an unmistakable way. Even Linda, who was four months pregnant and just beginning to show, had started to bother me about it. "When are you going to have a baby? Is anything wrong between you and him?" God help me if I ever got pregnant, my husband would surely comment on everything I put in my mouth, I'd get lectures night and day on the effect of bread on the purity of mother's milk.

"Ohio gozaimasu," Mrs. Imai called out as I walked up to her dry cleaning store.

Much more polite than just "Ohio." In Japanese the more polite you got the more syllables you added on to your words, the more words you added on to your sentences, the deeper you bowed. "Make Mrs. Imai your model," my husband used to say. "Mrs. Nakamura speaks men's Japanese." There was men's Japanese and women's Japanese and you had better know the difference, particularly if you were a woman. Men could be short, clipped, and abbreviated in their speech, but women had to go on and on, except with close friends, with whom they could speak in a more economical way. When I drank tea at the Imai's I'd lose track of all the extra syllables required to speak formal Japanese and end up dropping out of the conversation. My husband would translate until he got too involved in what everyone was saying to remember, and I'd smile and nod as if I was listening and nibble on the snacks laid out on the table for want of anything better to do. "Don't take the last rice cracker on the plate," my husband had warned. "It's not polite to eat the last section of orange." But would they even notice? And wouldn't they attribute my rudeness to a foreigner's ignorance?

"Not necessarily," Linda had said. "We're supposed to know better. We're married to Japanese."

This state of affairs, we had agreed, had its advantages. I stepped inside the dry cleaners and watched Mrs. Imai drape a woman's yellow silk suit in plastic as we chatted about nothing, and tried to remember what they were. All I could come up with for the moment was the camaraderie I experienced with Japanese when I told them I was married to one, a sense that I might almost become a member of the club. Japan was a reciprocal culture; Mrs. Imai plied me with tea and cookies and half-understood but patient conversations and all I ever did was bring her my husband's occasional dirty shirt. I ought to be spiffing up, I ought to be getting my wardrobe in order, I ought to be going to the department store to buy an Issey Miyake dress rather than an American whole wheat with a hard crust.

My stomach rumbled in hunger and alarm. The approaching train gave a sudden sharp whistle. I waved goodbye to Mrs. Imai, sprinted up the well-worn stairs to the station, and ran onto the train, remembering to set my face into the mask of impassivity everyone wore after the doors closed. Nobody made eye contact; looking straight ahead into nothing was the only way to maintain privacy in the crowd. I struggled not to search the blank faces for one that was animated, I clutched the train pole and let my eyes follow its long silver lines. My feet felt huge in their sneakers, besieged on all sides by the petite size five of the Japanese, like Gulliver surrounded by the Lilliputians. All I longed for these days was to sit around a campfire at Mt. Rainier, wearing the same clothes I'd worn for a hundred years, never going near a pair of gloves. I remembered that I'd once had more ambition in life than dressing a part. But what had it been? I closed my eyes and tried to dwell on something calming, brush paintings of wild mountain streams, the small figure of a man on a donkey, Issa's haiku about Mt. Fuji:

> Climb Mt. Fuji,
> O snail,
> but slowly, slowly.

"Never mind that the Japanese don't go on vacations, you definitely need one," Linda had said only days ago. "A vacation will restore your perspective on things. Tell him to leave his condoms at home and take you on one. How about Hawaii or Guam?"

"We'll climb Mt. Fuji," my husband had suggested when I brought up vacations. "It even looks like Mt. Rainier."

Never a man to do things halfway, he had taken to walking around the neighborhood with a compass cradled to his stomach, practicing his directions for our trip. Even now, when he should be cleaning the bathroom because it was his turn, he was likely peering at the topographical map, getting hungry looking at the heights we had to climb. "What a view from the top of Mt. Fuji on a clear day," he had said. "Even climbing in the mist is quite an experience." I'd never been afraid of mountains before, but now I was afraid of so many things.

"Ikebukuro Station," the train conductor announced over the loudspeaker in the politest of tones. "Kindly do not forget your belongings, and take care when you step off the train."

The train squealed to a stop. The Japanese businessmen exited in solemn procession, one dark suit after another. I clutched the pole a moment longer and imagined high winds sweeping climbers off the face of Mt. Fuji. It was better to fall than to go flying off the face of the earth with no warning. I wanted to slide down the rocky slopes, to have time to think of what was ahead during my descent. I didn't have the courage to bear an inevitable end, the abrupt change of perspective such finality requires. Till death do us part.

"Do you think about it sometimes?" I had asked Linda. "Living here all your life?"

"Yeah. Being an old lady, having to take the crowded train. Always being a foreigner. Not being able to carry on a really in-depth conversation with my kids."

"What do you mean?"

"Carol Tanaka said if you send them to a public school their language ability shoots way ahead of yours. By the time they hit adolescence, you can't really talk to them anymore."

I imagined our kids, two of them, standing next to the TV in a corner of the room with a cloth draped over their not quite black hair. No kids, I promised myself. First things first. Bread is the staff of life, my grandmother had said. Reaching into her barrel of flour. Punching down dough, watching it rise. Eating it is the next best thing to making it. I handed my ticket to the ticket taker. I walked into Ikebukuro department store to buy my bread, passing tofu floating in tubs of fresh water, a white-hatted chef who bowed to me from behind a stack of perfect rice cakes, a fishmonger in a clean apron laying out pink-fleshed fish and singing, "Oishii sakana de gozaimasu." I stopped at the entrance to the bakery and inhaled the smell of fresh bread. I picked up a tray. I said "pan, pan, pan." I lingered in front of the tortes, their fillings cleanly packed in the middle of two squares of sponge, the dusting of sugar like the powder I never wore on my cheeks. "Hada ga shiroi desu ne," Mrs. Nakamura used to say. "Your skin is so white." I grabbed a whole wheat from the loaves that lay cheek to cheek on the shelves, and took it to the counter to pay for it.

"Three thousand yen," the clerk said, sliding the loaf into a bag. I clamped it under my arm and stepped onto the crowded escalator going up to the first floor. The smell of fresh bread wafted through the air as the escalator rose, and the loaf was warm under my arm. I ignored the mannequins standing in insolent poses at the top of the stairs, their plastic forms draped with elegant dresses. I ignored polished counters and the floor's brash shine, I sailed past the salesladies' bows and out into the street.

I tore off a piece from my loaf. Every car in the street honked their horn. I popped the bread in, and closed my lips firmly. Pigeons swooped, their gray wings flapping. I imagined their little stomachs puffing out as the yeast expanded, their chi running wild through their tiny bird meridians, their cooing getting blocked in their throats. The taste of home flooded my mouth. The pigeons bowed their heads up and down, yes yes yes. I shared the rest of my bread.

Finding Land

It was an ordinary day until I met a woman named Linda in the snack aisle at Seibu Supermarket, where she was contemplating dried squid in a bag. "It goes well with beer," I said to her, assuming an instant bond since she was a foreigner too. In my relief at finding a countrywoman in the local supermarket, and one who, like me, was married to a Japanese, I ended up forgetting to buy milk, which only I would drink anyway, and ordering American coffee with her in a café while our groceries melted beside us in bags on the floor. She took a bite of her tiny slice of strawberry cake and said she'd been hungry since the moment she'd arrived in Japan eight weeks ago.

"It's the portions," I said consolingly. "Little portions for little people."

"And not enough frosting on the cake," she added.

We stared at each other, two large women across a toy-sized table in a room scarcely bigger than the treehouse of my childhood, in the sugar maple tree that stood in the big field where I caught butterflies, years ago, or so it seemed, in Cleveland. Afterwards I'd stuck them to a board with a pin. I was into collecting. "I'm twenty-four," I added, irrelevantly. I was large by being too tall, often thwacking my head on low doorways like a blind woman entering an unfamiliar room. A bump like the nub of a unicorn's horn grew on my head. At night my husband burned little moxibustion cones around its circumference in order to reduce the swelling and reminded me to duck going into rooms. Linda was a modest height, though she had hips and a bosom. I hoped she'd brought enough clothes with her to last her for a couple of years.

"After a while your stomach will shrink to the size of the portions," I said.

"Not mine. I'm pregnant."

She was sure not to have brought enough clothes. But at least her children would be the size of the Japanese, though it was doubtful they'd look like them, given the color of her hair. Mine would look almost Japanese, but their height would instantly betray their difference. Their exposed ankles would always be going red in the cold, their bony arms would stick out of their sleeves. My father-in-law still couldn't get over the fact that he barely came up to my shoulders. He had mentioned basketball, which he had watched—though he much preferred baseball—on national TV. He had asked my husband if I was going to grow anymore.

"She's stopped," my husband had said. "Good thing, because we've run out of closet space." I had to sleep with my feet in the closet. Otherwise I got cranky, because I couldn't stretch out my legs on the floor of our four-mat tatami room.

Linda chewed her last bite of cake. She took ten rice crackers out of her grocery bag and ate them. I ate three, and told her I didn't want to conceive. I used birth control religiously, I said. I slept with my diaphragm by my pillow, snug in its little pink box. If I got pregnant I'd grow large in two directions, three if you counted the nascent horn. During delivery I'd be lying on the table with my legs hanging off the edge, not that I'd be able to see them. And so I was waiting. (For what, I didn't know. The shrinkage of age?)

At this point Linda said, "Deborah, let's forget about cooking dinner and go find land."

"Find land?" I was still flat on my back on the delivery table, putting my feet in stirrups, about to strike the doctor in the nose as I bent my bony knees.

"Yeah, land. Like in, space. The buffaloes and all that." She plunged her hand into her grocery bag.

Perhaps she had a deficient education in geography, not unusual for many Americans, and imagined uncharted land in Japan, vast prairies as yet unexplored. Maybe she didn't even know she was on an island in the middle of the sea. Three seas—four if you included the Seto Inland Sea. Mountains that thrust up everywhere except on the great Kanto plain, spreading under us from Tokyo to Osaka, the Osaka plain, the Niigata plain, and a few more I couldn't remember that were up north in Hokkaido. I prepared to explain a few things to Linda, feeling satisfied that there were a few things that could be explained, as there were so many that couldn't. I took out the bilingual atlas I had purchased within my first few hours on this soil.

But with nary a glance at the beautiful picture of the islands of Japan on its cover, all reds and oranges and greens in the middle of three vast blue seas and one little narrow lighter-colored one, Linda withdrew the package of dried squid from her bag. She tore it open and cautiously sniffed it. She bit down into a flat, red-brown corner. She chewed and chewed and chewed and finally swallowed. "This squid's a tough sucker," she said. She licked her finger and pressed it over the crumbs on her plate. She carefully tipped the coffee on her saucer back into her cup and drank it. The waiter, swishing a pretty checked cloth over the next table and humming a popular tune, gave us a look as Linda tore open another package with her teeth.

"Do you mind?" she asked him with a disarming smile. He blushed and folded his towel and hurried behind the counter, where he dripped coffee and rattled cups and pretended not to stare. He was probably amazed that she liked Japanese snacks. I had been accosted once with a bean cake in my hand in Roppongi Station by a Japanese TV crew, who had interviewed me about my eating habits, and then aired it as a spot on the midnight news.

"Whatever these are they're easier to chew," Linda said. "Much, much easier. And they're sugared so they'll last for our trip. Have some."

I decided not to say a word to her about the Kanto plain, or the dearth of available land. Being humbled was a constant experience of life here. One felt smaller by the day and yet larger. Linda would too. Particularly in her condition. Who was I to dash her daring with a lecture about the four islands and three seas? The waiter couldn't be expected to understand that blood stirred in strange ways here, that hunger beset one at unexpected moments. Women who had once possessed sense and a bank account suddenly threw themselves into some Japanese man's arms. They ended up sleeping with their feet in the closet. They got pregnant despite their little pink box. It could happen to me.

I put the atlas in my lap, and popped a candied azuki bean into my mouth. I turned to the twenty-three wards of Tokyo, color-coded for convenience, with place names marked in English and Japanese. In Yoyogi Park, youth with dyed orange hair teased into stiff peaks cradled ghetto blasters and danced the grass into submission, pausing to neck on park benches when they wanted to rest their feet. In Shinjuku Park, smart-suited matrons of the city walked dogs named Shiro, little toy things that went yap yap yap and wagged fluffy tails. In Ueno Park, salarymen on their lunch hour reclined on blankets under cherry trees, drinking beer, eating take-out yakitori chicken with their fingers, and serenading office ladies with warbly and mournful songs about falling cherry blossoms. Even now, in the coffee shop, shamisens were being strummed as background music to expensive coffee and strawberry cake.

The Japanese were incurable romantics. The space romance occupied was in inverse proportion to the tiny piece of land upon which they lived. They rose before dawn on New Year's Day to greet the first sunrise of the year, formed clubs to compose poetry, and sang enka—those schmaltziest of tunes about loss and love best sung while wearing a kimono—at every important occasion. I closed my atlas and hummed a song about the guy rowing a boat with his girl inside, the one my husband sometimes sang to me in the bath. It went well with the background music, the plinkity plink plink of the shamisen strings. I saw my husband's long-lashed eyes flutter at me as he perched on the toilet seat because there wasn't enough room for both of us in the tub, while I, gloriously naked, drew my knees to my chest. He rested a book on them. He gazed at me across the steam. He recited haiku:

> In the drained fields
> how long and thin
> the legs of the scarecrow.

"We have provisions." Linda rummaged noisily in her grocery bag, interrupting poetry. "Yes indeed we do, even if some of them are raw. Christopher Columbus wouldn't have minded raw, so why should we? And then there's those little noodle stands everywhere." She plunked a five hundred yen coin down on the table. She crumpled up her napkin, threw it on her plate, and made for the door. I folded my napkin neatly, just as I'd seen the Japanese do, placed it on the table, and hastened after her bobbing grocery bag, hugging my own to my chest and making sure to nod at the waiter over the cabbage head I was going to use to make stew if I ever got back home.

"Come again," the waiter said.

I ducked my head and shot out the door. I ran to catch up to Linda. She hurried along as if she knew where she was going, walking close to the shop fronts, without a single look to either side. She swung her free arm with a great deal of vigor. "Adventure is so exciting," she said. I lengthened my stride, shooting past giggling schoolgirls with linked arms admiring their reflections in shop windows, and a man clodding slowly in his wooden sandals, on his way to the public baths with a bucket over his arm and a towel slung over his shoulder. Perhaps, I thought, my husband would choose a different kind of poetry if we fit into the bath together. His sentiment might vary if we occupied a larger space, a castle with many turrets, such as the one I'd seen on a distant velvet hilltop when we'd taken a train the length of the main island, or a farmhouse with a thatched roof standing beside terraced rice fields. I could call him at his clinic in Shibuya from some wayward station, like a wandering samurai, a ronin without lord or master, and tell him I was on a larger quest than cooking winter stew with cabbage and pumpkin.

The narrow street disappeared. A horse galloped by, waving the plume of its tail. I imagined my grocery bag flying out of my arms and coming to rest on the branch of a tree, a squirrel reaching its head inside to nibble.

"I have to go to the bathroom," Linda called over her shoulder. "Pee pee pee when you're pregnant and nothing else."

The vision of a mythical land, all green-velvet rolling hills and a many-turreted castle, vanished. I thought again of the delivery table, those stirrups just waiting for my feet. Housewives whizzed by on their errands, babies plastered to their backs. Tinkle, tinkle, tinkle, their little bicycle bells said.

"There's a bathroom in the station," I said, stepping up beside Linda. "But we have to buy a ticket first and pass through the gate."

"Hold this a minute. I'm going to get comfortable." Linda turned her back to the street, and undid the top button of her jeans. I held both bags close, and watched the sleek crowds part around us and hurry on their way up the station stairs. Japanese working women looked perfectly collected. I wondered if Linda had noticed that too. I couldn't imagine them weeping while slicing onions. They seemed entirely different from the housewives on their bicycles. They had mastered the art of fast walking on high heels. And yet, once they got married, they'd undergo a transformation. They'd quit work, or be forced to, and bear a baby within a year. They'd begin to look rumpled.

"Finished," Linda said, and twirled around twice. "Good. Looks like my zipper's gonna hold its position. Let's go!" She took her bag, and flew up the station stairs.

The train whistle blew. The announcer announced something in an amplified voice. A barrage of heels tapped the floor. The clerk at the newsstand slapped change into customers' palms along with their papers. People moved in purposeful blurs, hurrying to catch the train. What were we doing? Japan wasn't the remote Himalayas. We'd end up lost among buildings on a crowded street. We'd wander down aisles lined with discount electronic goods in Akihabara forever. We'd eat our way to the bottom of our grocery bags, and have to undo our zippers, and worst of all, we wouldn't find any land. There wasn't any, not the slightest bit of available space. I reached for the back of Linda's coat, but her forward momentum pulled it out of my grasp. She skidded to a halt at the ticket machines, and rested her free hand on the metal.

"I used my last coin to tip the waiter," she said. "That's what you get for going against custom." She took a package of dried seaweed out of her grocery bag and fanned herself. A Japanese woman pressed a button on the next machine, took out her ticket, and slid it between her teeth. She glanced at Linda, and then at me. She walked swiftly toward the gate, maneuvering around businessmen rushing with their coats flapping against their legs, and groups of schoolchildren with bulging black briefcases. Her slim maroon bag, embossed with the gold logo of a Ginza department store, swung gently by its handle from her ivory fingers. An edge of tissue paper swirled out of the top like a puff of whipped cream.

Linda turned a shade paler. She stared at the map above the ticket machines, at the train lines snaking in all directions. Chinese characters abounded, labeling place names unknown. "I'll have to learn how to read all those damn Chinese characters," Linda muttered. She drew her arms all the way around her bag and clasped her fingers. Her head drooped down toward her leafy lettuce.

"Where are we going anyways?" she asked in a small voice.

I swallowed the words of defeat I was about to utter, and pushed the cabbage head firmly into the depths of my grocery bag. It came to rest next to a block of Hokkaido butter.

"Getting around Japan is easier than it looks," I said. "Especially if you employ the Ouija-board method of decision making. Watch this."

Her head lifted. I crouched and sprang. My free arm extended upwards. The flat of my hand smacked the map. A mandarin orange sailed out of my hag.

"Amazing," a voice said in Japanese behind me. "She must play basket-oh baru."

I landed with a thud. "We're going to Me-something or other," I said, slipping coins into the ticket machine. "We'll change to a bullet train in Tokyo Station. It looks like it's somewhere south of here."

"Great. Terrific. That was a wonderful leap." Linda smiled at the middle-aged businessman whose gray hair was combed to cover the bald spot on his head as he placed the mandarin orange in her palm. The businessman bowed and hurried away. She tipped the orange into her grocery bag, and extended the package of dried squid.

"Trade you," she said.

I suddenly felt ridiculous carrying a grocery bag. Toshiro Mifune didn't carry a grocery bag. Instead, he swaggered around picking fights and speaking men's Japanese. Nevertheless, the grocery bag was a fact of life, and the land a mythical vision, a Me-something or other of no place and no name.

Linda shifted her bag to her hip. Something inside rattled like a saber. Whatever it was, I hoped she wouldn't eat it. "Are you ready to go? My bladder's gonna burst." She put her hand on her stomach.

"You okay? I mean, the baby and everything. Can you handle a trip?"

"I'm fine. Pregnancy is no big deal, once you get used to the little inconveniences. Besides, I've decided I don't have to wait until delivery for birth to begin. C'mon. I'd better pee before the train comes." We heard the clacking of the train wheels sounding in the distance. Linda's hair floated back like a banner. I thought of peninsulas beckoning from the sea, a butterfly on the wing, a sunset of rainbow colors throwing light in our faces. Land awaited. I faced forward. I dropped the squid in. I ran after Linda.

Later, in a lost corner of Tokyo Station, we stood holding our grocery bag, staring at the picture on a giant TV screen. A young girl strode about a stage, flinging her hair and singing off-key. "Well, will you look at that. She can't sing," Linda said, wiping off her mustache of milk. We were down to half a liter. At the rate she was going, we were going to have to find land with a cow on it. That could be a problem, unless we went to Hokkaido, which was another island entirely. I stared at the TV screen and tried to put the map out of my mind, the neat topographical picture I had of the four main islands of Japan, with lots of little ones speckled here and there like drops of cream. What we were searching for was mythical land, preferably with some kindly creatures on it, although all I could see for the moment were demons with scrunched-up faces and wicked grins. At various times throughout the morning, my neighbors had stood with their backs to the front door of our concrete apartment building that everyone called a "mansion" in Japanese-English for reasons I couldn't discern, tossing dried soybeans over their shoulders and chanting "Demons go out, gods come in!" "It's to protect their homes from bad luck," my husband said before he ran to catch his train. "It's bean-throwing day," he had added, as if that explained everything.

"She was hired for her looks," I said about the girl on the TV screen. "I guess it doesn't matter if she has talent."

"She's just a kid. What a terrible existence. She looks underfed and stressed out to me."

She turned her back to the screen, and took another sip from her carton. Citing ancient sources, my husband claimed that milk spoiled in the intestine and drained one's life force. But here was Linda, ready to have a baby. What was she supposed to do, nurse it on green tea?

"Remind me not to let my kid go in for something like that," Linda said. "People are already telling me how beautiful mixed babies look. I want my children to have normal lives." She took the mandarin orange out of her grocery bag and set it against the wall under the TV screen. "I knew this would come in handy. It's an offering for her. I know, it's weird, but it makes me feel better about leaving her in there. Are you ready? I'd better pee again before we go."

We found a bathroom and then walked up the platform stairs. A conductor waved us aboard with a white-gloved hand. Linda drew a carrot from her bag as the train sped out of the station. She crunched and stared out the window. The salaryman next to us yawned above his newspaper. A cow's eyes gazed mournfully from the page. When I took the train with my husband, he read instructional tidbits to me from his Oriental medicine books about how to balance my heart meridian. In romantic moments, he held my wrist and practiced pulse diagnosis. Right now, while we were seeking land, he was at his clinic, inserting acupuncture needles into somebody's foot or prescribing herbal medicine.

"Which way do you face when you use a Japanese-style toilet?" Linda asked.

"You go by the little feet on the floor," I said.

"Oh. I thought they were decorative. I was facing the wrong way." The man turned the page of his paper. The cow's eyes disappeared and were replaced by the stern face of the prime minister. "He's suffering from fatigue," my husband often said when he saw his national leader on TV. "He needs a good shiatsu treatment." The prime minister seemed to be looking directly at the huge photograph of the couple languishing in hot spring waters and smiling pleasantly; it sat above the shelf where everyone kept their briefcases. "Take the Japan National Railways to relaxation," were the words inscribed in a cloud of steam. In other advertisements, goggle-eyed scuba divers watched fish in Okinawa, and skiers in fluorescent green outfits whizzed down mountain slopes, snow flying from their heels. Couples strolled down paths lined with cherry trees, on honeymoon trips to Kyushu.

The salaryman flipped over his newspaper, without once lifting his head. Why should he care about a trip to Kyushu? He probably hadn't gone on a real vacation since his honeymoon. At most, salarymen had five or six days off at New Year's, and a few more during the Obon holiday in midsummer. Even then, they were expected to visit their ancestral villages. They didn't have the freedom to go anywhere they pleased. They were sacrifices for the economic miracle, record exports and a strong yen.

Their wives were too. My husband had his own acupuncture clinic, but he still couldn't go away with me for more than a few days. "Salarymen are my clients," he had said. "I have to keep *their* hours. When I went to Nepal, I lost business. But at least I found you."

"I'm going to have trouble squatting when I get bigger," Linda said. "I'll either have to find a Western-style toilet or hold it in."

"Do you have to go again?"

"Not yet."

"I think we're almost there."

I slid the atlas out of my purse, and turned it to the special maps at the back that marked where wild bladderwort grew and wisteria bloomed, where cranes migrated and white storks nested. Wildcats roamed one of the tiny Okinawan islands.

"Where did you get that? Can I see? Cool! A map of castle ruins! And here's one showing stone Buddhas!" Linda set her bag at her feet and turned pages. She took another bite of her carrot. Could I help her find what she was looking for? And what was I looking for? I didn't know. "You were looking for me," my husband had joked when I'd met him last year on a trip to the Himalayas. The recklessness of youth had inspired me to go trekking in the mountains in my sneakers. My trekking party ran into his at fifteen thousand feet above sea level, where our respective guides watched in alarm as he burned cones formed from mugwort leaves on my arches.

"Good thing I carry my moxibustion kit with me everywhere," he had said. "You could have lost your toes to frostbite. Don't shriek."

We'd gotten married. It was easier to get a visa if we tied the knot, and I wanted to be with him. Even so, the Japanese authorities had put me on a six-month probationary period. At the end of it, I'd get another six months, then a year's visa, then three, the visa officer had said, holding up three fingers. "Carry your passport with you everywhere," he had instructed. "In case a policeman stops you on the street."

"How did you meet your husband?" I asked Linda.

"He was attending my college in Texas. I kept inviting him over for brunch. Seduction accompli over steak and eggs. Now it's a more exotic menu. What's your story? You're kidding! Smooches in the Himalayas! A mountaintop proposal! How romantic!"

"Yes and no. It's one thing to fall in love, but another to come live in this place. Sometimes I wonder how it happened."

"Do you really?" Linda swallowed the last of her carrot. "It's easy to explain. Mine's handsome, and yours applied the heat when you needed it. Just remember your toes. No, but seriously, I know what you mean. Sometimes I wonder what I got myself into, especially since I got pregnant almost the second I got off the plane. Well, not exactly. I had to go through customs first. You're wise to wait."

"I'm scared of the whole idea," I said. "Plus I'm trying to learn how to read. So far I've memorized one hundred and fifty Chinese characters. Still, it's not enough to be able to read the newspaper. You have to know eight hundred characters, plus the two native syllabaries."

"Golly. My kid will probably learn to read before I do. Maybe something else besides procreating is in store for you. You might produce scholarly works on geography, while I become an explorer. Just don't audition to be a bombshell on TV. They go in for foreigners."

"I'm too tall to be a leading lady," I said. "I have to stoop to kiss my husband."

"Lucky man," Linda giggled. "He gets a breast-level view." She peered out the window. "Geez, this train is moving."

I joined Linda at the window, but the train moved so swiftly that all we saw were brief gleams as the sun caught windows, a blur of concrete, a factory appearing and disappearing. What would we see when we got to where we were going? None of the Japanese were watching the scenery. They read books or newspapers, or slept with their heads laid back against their seats. They stared straight ahead without looking at anything. They were lost in thought, or perhaps they thought nothing. "You maintain privacy in the crowd by keeping to yourself," my husband had said. "You'll see, you'll learn how to do it. You'll get used to it after a while." But the hush frightened me. Since I couldn't shrink to the size of the Japanese, would I become quiet instead?

"Is this your first time taking the bullet train?" the man next to us asked in English. He lowered his newspaper. We stared at him over the pages. I felt my mouth fall open. He looked like an ordinary Japanese salaryman. Not at all like someone who would strike up a conversation with two complete strangers. He caught my eye, smiled, and bowed deeply. His rounded back recalled the picture I had seen of the alluvial fans in the Nobi plain, sculpted slopes intersected by verdant valleys and flowing rivers. My heart lifted. I smiled and bowed too.

"Yes, it is our first time," Linda said, setting her bag at her feet. "And it's great, except it's really hard to see anything out the window."

"It gets easier when the train slows down near the station," the man said when he was upright again. He reached for the shelf above us, and put his newspaper into his briefcase. "Forgive me for bothering you, but I was listening to your English."

"Oh, God," I said.

"Not the words. Just the English. I'm a nosy man. My wife tells me so often. It's a good trait, I think. But not for Japanese, she says."

"I don't mind," Linda said. "You're the first Japanese who has ever started a conversation with me in public."

"They're shy people. They think you cannot speak Japanese."

"It's true," Linda said.

"Also, they think they cannot speak English. I mean, we think. Me, too, I think so. But, practice, practice. There's no other way. Speak boldly. Not like the Japanese. But I'm Japanese." He laughed. He took a handkerchief out of his pocket, and polished his glasses. His dark eyes twinkled. "When I speak English, I imagine I'm somebody new. Mr. Paul Newman, for instance."

"His aunt lives in my hometown," I said. "I saw him with her in a restaurant once." It had been a Jewish deli, of all places, Corky and Lenny's, where I'd been sitting with my grandma, who was speaking Yiddish to my mother because she didn't want me to understand what she was saying, and taking angry sips of her matzo ball soup. She hadn't recognized Paul Newman. The last movie she had seen was *Fiddler on the Roof*. She was too busy gossiping, probably about me. What was I doing moving to Japan with a foreigner I'd met on that crazy trip? She was sure there wasn't a synagogue in the whole place.

"Yes? Truly? So you see my resemblance to Mr. Newman?" The man beamed.

"Yeah. Yeah, I do." I needed to be someone new, too, I thought. Being Deborah Rosenboom just wasn't enough anymore.

"Me too," Linda said. "You've got that movie star smile."

"Oh, I'm happy man. I have two fans on this train."

"We're going to a peninsula, aren't we? At least I hope I read the map right." I set down my bag, and opened my atlas.

"*Miura kaigan*? Sorry, speak English, Mr. Newman! I mean, Miura peninsula! You're going there? It's my home place! Great land! Superb territory! Best view in Nippon!" He touched his finger fondly to the map, opened his mouth, and sang in a light tenor:

That mountain is high,
and I can't see Miura kaigan.
How I love Miura kaigan!
How I hate that mountain!

"I translated this into English. Do you like it? It's even better in the shower, but not bad on the train, too. Oh! Look!" He stood on his tip-toes, and leaned closer to the window. All of the passengers around us stared at him in astonishment. Some bent their heads to the windows, or exchanged amused glances and a few friendly words. I ducked under the bar that ran the length of the ceiling and pressed my face to the glass. Suddenly I felt I was up in my maple tree, peering through the leaves that had turned to gold and were swirling upwards at the wind's touch. I was watching the last flight of the butterflies. Their migration. Their escape from my net. The glass was soothing, a cool breeze against my cheeks. What did it matter what language we spoke? The best of us would be a blend, a mixture like Linda's baby, like the man beside us, who was both Mr. Newman and a Japanese. The sea stretched before us. Blue waves rolled against the shore.

"We can see the peninsula!" the man exclaimed. "And nice ocean, and some view!" He pointed out landmarks. He talked excitedly, mixing Japanese with English. He told us everything we could see on the peninsula, naming birds and fish and different kinds of seaweed, and then telling us where to find a rock shaped like a whale's tail on the beach. "You can sit down and have your picnic," he said. "Good things to eat in there, don't you?" He pointed to the clouds in the sky, and taught us how to say their shapes in Japanese. The train glided into the station. The doors swished open. Passengers scattered, checking watches and lighting cigarettes.

Numbers flashed above us on the board. We swept up our bags, and ran down the stairs together.

"That way to the beach," the man pointed. "Only fifteen minutes by slow walking. Oh, yes! You'll see the sunset. So-o-o beautiful. So-o-o great. So-o-o spectacular. With colors like a peacock's tail." He lifted his hand in the air and spread his fingers. He turned his hand this way and that. "See? Can you imagine?"

"Yes," we said.

The Hazards of Golf

Linda's baby is three weeks overdue.

She walks behind me. She is saying things I can't quite hear over the street noises: shopkeepers calling greetings to each other as their day begins, the rattle of metal awnings going up over doors. It's eleven a.m. and housewives bicycle their groceries home. Their husbands are at work. Linda's husband has forgotten to tie her shoes. She juts out in front and can't bend over to do it herself. The laces flap when she walks. I'm afraid she's going to trip on them, but I'm more afraid of a golf club coming out of nowhere to bash her on the head. I read about that last week in the *Japan Times*. A businessman who had come home from work early, out practicing his golf swing on the street, knocked a housewife in the head with his club. She was on her bicycle. She died and fell off.

I imagine the businessman standing with his feet planted apart as they do when they're golfing, his eyes fixed on an imaginary ball. Aim, swing. His wife would have been inside making his dinner, feeling happy because he was home early. It didn't actually say anything about his wife, but I'd just read the first two paragraphs of the article before the phone rang. It was Linda calling. Of course it was Linda. She says she can sense me the moment I walk in the door, but she gives me time to hang up my coat, take a look at the paper, begin to run the water for my bath.

"Hi," I said into the receiver, knowing it was her. Sachio moved about the kitchen as I talked to her, getting my dinner in its bowls. A separate bowl for everything. The rice in china, pale blue with white edges, the soup in lacquered wood, the tofu fresh and quivering on its small black plate.

"The baby hasn't been born yet," Linda said.

The cooked white radish in the soup looked like golf balls. I wasn't going to eat them.

"When will the baby be born?" Linda asked.

We're on our way to the doctor's to find out. He's the one who speaks English at the Catholic hospital in Iidabashi. He'll measure her cervix and report on its diameter. I'm not sure how they do that. Sometimes they sling a measuring tape around her middle and tell her she's too fat. She argues that she's a Western woman and Western women gain more weight in pregnancy. They've heard that one before; they get a lot of English-speaking women there because of the English-speaking doctor. I don't think she says it anymore; she doesn't really care. At this point she just wants the baby out. She'll keep the fat, but get the baby out. She says this to me several times. I'm listening, but I'm not the one who can do anything. She has asked them to induce her, but they won't do it unless the baby's in distress. That's what they say, "in distress." Linda's distressed all the time. She doesn't even mind about her shoelaces.

"I've got to tie them," I turn around and say to her. I can hear the distant sound of the train announcer at the station, bells going off as the train comes in.

"Tie them at the station. We'll be late if we don't catch the 11:30 express."

The baby is pressing against her stomach and the small of her back. I'm afraid it's blowing up like a balloon. The baby is fine, the English-speaking doctor told her on her last visit. The–baby–is–fine. He said it twice, pausing between the words, enunciating for Linda as though she doesn't speak English or is hard of hearing. I imagine the baby emerging from Linda, floating towards the ceiling. The umbilical cord tethering it to her. The lights of the delivery room bright in its face. When the doctor cuts the cord, the baby will float away.

"She's more likely to drop like a stone," Linda says when I tell her this. "This is one heavy baby. Either that, or my fat weighs a lot."

She walks steadily behind me. I'm relieved to see that her feet are keeping out of the way of her shoelaces, but it would only take a second to tie them. I wonder why she won't let me tie them. Keep your feet on the ground, she's always telling me. We're in a different world here. But the baby being overdue is driving her crazy. She's can't see her feet any-more; her mind is centered on her middle.

"Who's going to take care of the baby if anything happens to Linda?" I asked Sachio before he left for work this morning. The housewife who was killed by the golf club left two small children. Linda's planning on three. If they're all late like this, I won't be able to take it.

"Linda will be fine," he said. "Japan's a very safe place to have a baby."

It's not what I meant, but I don't repeat my question. Sachio isn't a demonstrative man, but he cares. Linda says the same thing. The infant mortality rate is lower here than it is in the States. National health insurance, so every woman can get good prenatal care, no unnecessary cesareans. A better place to have a baby than the U.S., she said, adding, when are you going to have one?

My mother-in-law is always wondering about it too, but she's too polite to ask. "It's just that the box the condoms come in is so pretty," I said to Linda. She didn't know what to make of that. Light blue with two silver birds and two dusk blue roses on it. I can never resist those boxes when the door-to-door condom salesman comes. Then you have to use them or they pile up. There's no storage in Tokyo apartments, not the slightest bit of extra space. I wouldn't have that job for anything. He does it so well, he's discreet, but he blushes slightly when I answer the door.

"I wonder if the Japanese housewives do that to him," I say to Linda. She has paused for a moment to catch her breath.

"Do what to who?"

I explain about the blushing condom salesman.

Linda looks appalled. "I would never buy those from a door-to-door salesman."

"That's why you're pregnant."

"It was planned," she says, and starts walking again.

"Oh, right."

The first time he came to the door I had no idea what he was sell-ing, although the word for condom is the same in Japanese as in English. It's called a "foreign loan word." What made it difficult to understand is that he pronounced it with the Japanese vowel sounds, which are like the Spanish vowel sounds if you know Spanish. That's what my Japanese teacher said, and it wasn't helpful for me, because I'd had French. The salesman had to take one out and show it to me because the picture on the box wasn't at all like the pictures on contraceptives in the States. No men and women holding hands, no long hair blowing in the wind, only roses and silver birds flying in a cloudless blue sky.

"I like these boxes better than the ones in the States," I said to Sachio when I first bought one. "What's the big deal about long hair anyway?"

"Long hair is a symbol of a woman's beauty," he said.

He has an answer for everything.

When Sachio gets mad at me he tells me he wants a Japanese wife. Long black hair and all. Mine's dark brown and short and frizzes when it rains. A Mrs. Kobayashi cuts it. In junior high I had it long, and Benjamin Arnovitz used to tell me I looked like a witch. Last I heard, he still lives in Cleveland and wears a yarmulke to cover his bald spot. A row of young Japanese women sit in Mrs. Kobayashi's beauty parlor with their long hair wrapped in something that looks like saran wrap. They flip through women's magazines or lean back with their eyes half-closed. They have beautifully painted nails.

"You have lovely hair," Mrs. Kobayashi says, and snips. "Lovely" is hard for her to pronounce. All those "l's." I don't argue with her. She practices good customer relations.

"What's that wrapping do for their hair?"

But she places the dryer in her assistant's hand and bustles off. He forgets to put the setting on cool. Hot air makes my hair frizz, but I don't tell him, because he'll apologize profusely, more than is necessary. He's about nineteen, with orange hair that slumps over his head except where he's stiffened it with cream. He bends over and directs hot air at the side of my head. I can see he's going black at the roots. Mrs. Kobayashi is unwrapping one young woman's hair. My ear burns. I can't help holding my breath.

Free of the wrapping, her hair sends off sparks. It's so glossy it might catch on fire.

If Sachio had married a Japanese woman, he might have had a baby by now. One with black hair that sticks up in tufts. To be fair, Sachio says he doesn't need a baby to prove he's a man.

Linda's baby was conceived in the Meguro Emperor Love Hotel, a fifteen-minute walk from Meguro station on the Yamanote train line.

Linda and I made a special trip to see the hotel when she was in her fifth month and feeling great. Koki had brought her there as a surprise. I couldn't believe my eyes when I saw the turrets; it looks just like a castle from the outside. Inside they made love in the Royal Couple's Luxury Boudoir, fifteen thousand yen to rent by the hour, decorated with floor-to-ceiling mirrors, an emperor and empress's throne upholstered in red velvet, and a canopy that encircled a mammoth bed. Did they stand over your bed with crossed swords? I wanted to know. And did you ever sit on your throne? Without answering either question, she confessed she laughed throughout the whole thing. It's one thing to make love in a place so kitschy, another to conceive there, a third to laugh about it. Linda described the condom dispenser in the bathroom. It was shaped like a crown. You placed a coin in a slot at the top and a fake jewel popped open in the front. The condom came out in a small purple envelope. Obviously Koki didn't use it, because Linda says she's sure she conceived the baby that night.

Sometimes there's a knock at my door and it's the Mormons. They're all over Tokyo, polite, handsome blond men from Utah dressed in white shirts with plain dark ties. They speak perfect idiomatic Japanese and bicycle around the streets of Niiza City where I live, stopping to knock on doors and dispense literature to housewives about the free English classes they run at their local church. To the Japanese they're exotic and wholesome. Unlike my condom salesman, they look disappointed when I answer the door. They know they can't sell me anything. I take their literature anyway; it's free. If only they knew what else I was getting at the door.

We've made it safely to the station without a golf club injury. Now Linda just has to walk up the steps. She pauses at the first and places her hand on the rail.

"Japanese women don't yell when they give birth."

"How do you know?"

"Koki told me."

"How does he know?"

"That's what I said. He said everyone knows that."

Linda has gone up only two steps during this exchange. We should have taken a taxi. It's a common ploy of our husbands to defend their logic by the everyone–does–it–this–way argument. By "everyone" they mean "all Japanese." We're not Japanese. We use that in our defense, but it doesn't let us off the hook.

"You have to cut the carrots at an angle like this," Sachio said after we were first married.

"Why?" He had never said a word to me about my carrots when we were living in the States.

"Everyone does it like this." He took the knife out of my hand and began to slice.

I gave up cooking. Linda was envious.

She goes up another step. "He'll be embarrassed if I yell during delivery." At this rate we'll never get up these steps. I can hear a train coming in, and women run around us to catch it. The men are all at work. Never mind, we'll catch the next one. Linda's a yeller anyway. She yells into her washing machine when it's in the spin cycle. The agitation of the machine covers her noise. In Tokyo we all wash outdoors, on our verandas where the washing machines are kept. It has gotten around about Linda and her washing machine among the Filipino girls. They're in the *Japan Times* too now and then, in feature articles about the yakuza tricking them into a life of prostitution over here. I want to speak to them, but I don't know what to say. The Mormons don't go near them either. There's not much to entertain them in life, so Linda doesn't mind if they watch her yell at her spinning clothes. They wait on the street for Linda to appear, looking up at her second floor veranda, giggling together, saying things in what must be Tagalog. Yelling's the same no matter what language it's in, but they're not yellers. I think Linda should wait until the rinse cycle to yell, when the water is streaming quietly over the clothes and the sound of her own voice can be heard.

We've reached the top step. I buy the tickets and give one to Linda.

"I'm almost sorry I invited him to be at the delivery," Linda says.

"It'll be fine."

She had to write a letter to the hospital, petitioning them to let Koki into the delivery room. It's an irregular procedure, the hospital wrote back. We don't usually let the husbands go in. I would think if he's not around she could yell all she wants, but it's too late, the hospital has already given their permission. She wants me there too; she's a woman who doesn't mind an audience to a few good screams, but Koki wouldn't have it.

We stand at the platform, waiting for the train. Houses crowd just beyond the tracks and a summer breeze stirs the washing on the lines. I'm hoping she won't look too closely at the washing, but she does.

"Diapers," she groans. Hanging on the line stretched across her room, growing stiff and cold in winter. She's demanding he buy a dryer. Almost nobody has a dryer in Tokyo. Well, she will. It's that or disposable diapers. He had a fit. What kind of a mother would use disposable diapers? I wouldn't have believed it except that Sachio said the same thing when I asked him about it. No disposable diapers. You have to use cloth.

"You don't even have a baby," I snapped. "You could change your mind by that time."

"Never," he said. "When in Rome." He knows too much English for his own good, and then he wonders why I scream at him.

When Linda isn't complaining about the baby being overdue she worries about diapers. The baby will still be in them come winter. How will she get them dry? They'll be hanging on the line in her living room, drying reluctantly in the cold damp air, shrinking into themselves like little old men. The baby will shriek with cold when she puts them on her bottom. His bottom, Koki says. He's sure it's going to be a boy. Maybe even two boys. If you're having twins, you can be as big as she is. Just what is she eating, the doctor wants to know. Persimmons, she says, but he doesn't listen. Persimmons, fermented beans, heaping bowls of rice, the crisp snap of radish pickles in her mouth. Far too many rice crackers. This pregnancy business is salty, she says, but to me, not the doctor. We can tell each other everything. Words fly uncensored out of our mouths. English is a bold language, Japanese a careful one. Our husbands have silky smooth skin and very little body hair. You could bury your hands in their skin; it's that soft. Koreans are supposed to have even softer skin, Sachio has told me. And of course he says it, too; a Korean wife would be nice, for her skin.

"The last time I went to the doctor, he told me that sex might help me deliver sooner," Linda says. A loud whooshing noise I can't quite place drowns out her next words.

"He said that? Really?"

"His delivery was more discreet. Like your condom salesman's." She gives a great hoot. I'm startled and look her over. Is it the baby this time? No, it appears to be a belly laugh, one that she forgets to hide behind her hand. Japanese women always laugh behind their hands. It's not polite to show your teeth. Even a smile gets covered.

"Well, is Koki interested?" I wanted to know.

"I can't even get him to remember to tie my shoes."

The whooshing noise is coming from a vacuum truck parked in front of a small house near the train tracks. Sachio wanted to be a vacuum truck driver when he was a child. He loved the noise it made, and he wanted to carry the long hose and put it down the toilet. He's ended up in robotics, designing mini-golf courses inside fancy hotels. It's much more lucrative, and you don't have to cope with the smell. It may even save lives. Businessmen who are tempted to practice their swings in Tokyo's great out-of-doors are putting instead on Sachio's golf courses, on the sections of floor that can be moved up or down to simulate hills or valleys. It was quite a feat, designing those, but it didn't save that housewife's life. Her husband is suing the businessman for five million yen, for the loss of her labor to him and his children. I wonder if Linda and I are worth that to our husbands.

When I'm having a good day, I think it's Sachio who keeps me going. On a bad day, I know it's Linda. I can't even begin to explain what it's like here to my friends back in the States. They always complain I don't say much in my letters, but it's impossible to give them enough of the context.

"Do you think our friends are having the same troubles in America?" Linda asks, as if reading my mind.

"At least they're not getting decked by golf clubs."

Now I've done it. Linda looks alarmed. I haven't told her about the golf club killing. She puts her hand on her back.

"What do you mean?"

"I was just thinking about the hazards of golf." It's a lame explanation, but Linda's back is obviously distracting her, and she drops the subject to rub it. I try to think how to take her mind off her back. I've tried reading to her before, and I do have a couple of the *Japan Times* sticking out of my shoulder bag that I was going to read while Linda was in getting measured. They all have articles about the golf club killing. It must be a

big human-interest story in the English-speaking community. I'm surprised Linda hasn't mentioned it, because she reads the paper, but she's
said she can't concentrate these days. I take a quick glance at the current
golf club story. The businessman was swinging a new Mizuno iron that
his boss had given him. Meaning the golf club, but irons make me think
of white shirts, and how I've convinced Sachio to get his ironed at the
dry cleaners instead of at home. Linda is still working on Koki, so I don't
want to read anything to her that will remind her of Koki's white shirts
spread out on her board. There are other articles I can read to her. For
example, Elsie and Fumiko's column about women working in the business world in Tokyo. Linda always gets a kick out of that column. This
one's all about not showing your upper arm. The Japanese consider the
upper arm sexy, and they won't take you seriously if you're sleeveless. No
wonder the condom salesman blushed. Short sleeves are okay. This is fas-
cinating stuff, and Linda seems to be listening. I start to really get into it
but she has an outburst.

"Oh, hell, nothing seems to fit me anymore."

I've seen her so often throughout her pregnancy that I've had time
to notice the change in her girth. But Sachio, who saw her once at four
months and then again at eight, says she's grown one tatami mat size in
width and he doesn't know how she and Koki fit into their four mat bedroom anymore. It was a mean thing to say. She's beautiful. I'm always
telling her that, and I tell her now.

"My breasts are killing me," she says. She was never good at taking
compliments, even before she got pregnant. She puts her hands under
her breasts for support. It's then I notice Mrs. Saito standing down the
platform. She's one of my private English students, a doctor's wife with
an unusually large house by Tokyo standards and daughters who are
planning trips to Australia and Guam. She's staring at Linda.

Linda is wearing a purple maternity dress that her mother sent
from Dallas after Linda tried to find one she could fit into at Ikebukuro
Department Store. It was awful, the salesladies so polite as they always
are, not giving the slightest hint that she was as big as an elephant and
her shoes were untied. They bowed lower than they usually do when she
left the store. Why don't you tie my shoes while you're down there, she
wanted to say. You would think Koki could remember to tie a good knot.

She enjoyed it when she could still see his back sloping down and his head bent over her feet, but now she wanted to get it over with. He said, "What's the hurry? If I don't tie knots in them they'll come undone when you're halfway to the vegetable shop." Why don't you go to the vegetable shop, she wanted to ask. You would think he would notice she was nine months and three weeks pregnant and it was getting difficult to shop, knots or no knots.

Mrs. Saito is coming towards us, taking small steps in shiny white shoes. She's wearing a tailored linen summer suit the color of cantaloupe, cool and fresh in the August air. Her eyes are still on Linda and a smile dazzles her face.

"Good morning," she says in her gentle voice. I'm surprised she's come up to us like this. She might if I were alone, but two foreigners together would surely scare her away. Maybe she just wants to practice her English on somebody new. We both say hello, and Linda extends her hand cordially towards Mrs. Saito while I introduce her. Good thing we covered handshakes in English class. In Japan you always bow. Mrs. Saito takes Linda's hand and bows. All ground is covered.

"Pleased to meet you," she says. Perfect! That can give my students trouble, don't ask me why. Linda is beaming away. She looks happier than I've seen her look all morning. Mrs. Saito lets go of her hand and murmurs, "Do you mind?" A deceptively simple phrase, so nicely rendered! Then she kneels by Linda's white sneakers, Japanese size nine, and ties the laces. First the one on the right shoe, then the one on the left. Neat, solid, sturdy bows, perfectly balanced between one loop and the other. Then she brushes bits of dirt off the tops. Linda's shoes haven't gotten this much attention in weeks.

The train arrives and we board it together. The car is almost empty. There are two older women dressed for shopping who give us a quick glance before placing their purses on their laps. A young woman flips her waist-length hair, sits near the door, and opens a manga comic book. Mrs. Saito and Linda chat quietly. The train moves off with a rumble. I'm thinking of the ribs on the Slingwinkies, the newest brand of condoms that my salesman sold me, and watching the familiar scenery passing by. Suddenly Linda cries out. I leap to my feet. Mrs. Saito jumps up too.

Our arms go protectively around Linda. She rises in their circle, purple and majestic. "My waters have broken," she announces.

We all look at the puddle on her seat. Mrs. Saito takes a handkerchief out of her suit pocket, unfolds it, and spreads it over the water. The two older women wipe Linda's dress and the younger woman helps Mrs. Saito with the puddle. Linda settles herself back down on a dry place on the seat. She looks just like I imagine the Empress Meguro would look if she were a pregnant white woman. She's calm with relief. She isn't about to yell for anything, she's saving it for later, so I do it for her. The Japanese women look shocked, and then they laugh. Not one bothers to hide her teeth.

The Cherry Blossom Report

A few days after my friend Kazuko left her husband and came to stay with me, the national news started reporting on the blooming of cherry trees across Japan. We sat on the tatami mat floor in front of the TV, eating sugar glazed doughnuts and watching a man in a suit pointing at a map of Japan as he explained where the cherry blossoms were blooming, where they were about to bloom, and where no buds had yet appeared, an accounting of flowering, of the promise of flowering, which was given as much weight as the day's headline news.

"I'd like to go to Holland," Kazuko said, brushing crumbs off her shirt. "I'd like to see the tulips. I'm tired of cherry blossoms." She had found a note from a woman in the pocket of her husband's pants when he left them lying on the floor. She and her husband never fought, but the marriage just slipped away. She didn't think he cared much for the woman he was seeing. She could tell this from the woman's note, from its pleading tone.

"If you keep reading that note you'll have it memorized," I said.

"I memorized it the first time I read it." Kazuko cracked open the veranda door, letting in a warm breeze. The night before, while she sat up smoking in the other room, I'd dreamt I was walking along the Ochiai River. My ankle was still in its splint, but I kept walking through the pain. When I reached the place in the river where the black-crowned night heron came to fish I realized I didn't have my crutches. I was walking, and I wasn't supposed to do any weight bearing, but it felt so good.

"Tear up the note," I said to Kazuko. "Tear it up in little pieces and throw them away."

My best friend Linda came out of my little kitchen with a pot of tea. She was pregnant again, with her third. "Happily pregnant," she had said when she broke the news. She poured us tea. The first sip burned. "I put sake in it," she announced before I could ask her what she had done to the tea. "Hot sake. Didn't you smell me heating it?" She sat, heavily, on the one and only chair in our eight mat room.

"Where did you get the sake?"

"I raided Koki's secret stash. Look at that," she pointed at the TV. "The cherry blossoms have already bloomed in Okinawa."

"They always bloom first in Okinawa. It's warmer down there."

"Wouldn't it be interesting if the blossoms bloomed in reverse?" Linda said. "If they started blooming in Hokkaido, and went south from there?"

"Or if they never fell to the ground," I said. "If they always stayed on the trees."

"I'd have to leave Japan," Kazuko said. "I wouldn't be able to stand it. Immortal cherry blossoms."

I took another sip of tea. "It's not bad, but it could use some sugar. I'm just kidding," I said when Linda started to rise from her chair. "When I first came here Sachio told me twenty times the Japanese never put sugar in green tea until I finally stopped doing it myself."

"They're all nuts," Linda said. "I love them but they're nuts." She looked at Kazuko. "Present company excepted." But Kazuko, sitting now with her back against the door frame, seemed to be listening to the sound of a piano from down the street, someone practicing scales with a firm touch. It was a girl, most likely, though probably not Rei-chan, the fourteen year old I tutored in English, whose mother was having her instructed in piano and flower arranging and other ladylike arts. Whenever I coaxed Rei-chan to say something in English, she trembled and turned red and stared at the floor.

"My mother gave me kimonos when I got married," Kazuko said. "A married woman is supposed to have kimonos. And children. She always thought something was medically wrong with me or my husband that kept us from having children. She never would have understood if I told her it was my choice."

"They're a lot of work," Linda said.

"I wear a kimono every New Year's so my mother can see they aren't always folded away. I won't do that anymore."

"On my wedding day it took two women plus my mother-in-law to tie me into my kimono," Linda said. "They didn't seem to notice I had a bulge at the waist, or maybe they thought they could just flatten it down with that whatchamacallit sash thing."

"Óbi," I said.

"Right, óbi."

"Maybe if we'd had children, he wouldn't have cheated on me," Kazuko said.

"That wouldn't have stopped him," Linda snapped. I froze with my hand over the box of doughnuts, then took another sugar glazed, my third, and passed the box to Linda. I didn't know what else to do. "I've dropped the boys at my mother-in-law's," she had told me when she called. "They need a break from me." I watched her balance a doughnut on top of her big round belly. Maybe she was running away from home, too.

The flower reporter on the TV kept up his enthusiastic patter. He swirled his long pointer around a map of Okinawa Island and the screen filled with shots of trees heavy with blooms. People strolled along park paths, looking upwards at the blossoms, clicking with their cameras. They lounged beneath the trees. They ate bean sweets in the shape of cherry blossoms. I even saw a woman licking her fingers, something I normally never saw women here do.

"I'm glad the cherry trees aren't blooming yet in Tokyo," Kazuko said. "I don't want to be here when they do."

"The cherry blossom season will be over in Okinawa by that time," I said. "You can go there. We can all go there. Be in a different culture."

"We are in a different culture," Linda said.

"I'd rather go to Holland," Kazuko said. "I want to see the tulips, and the windmills, and the wooden shoes."

"Until I moved to Japan, I'd never been further than Houston," Linda said.

"We're not in Kansas any longer," she had remarked the first time we watched the cherry blossom report. That was in the old days, when we were newcomers to Japan, when she was suckling her first, who had been ten pounds at birth. When we were both reasonably happy. Linda still was, I thought, but why had she dropped her boys off at her mother-in-law's and come here? She always said there was nothing to do in Hibarigaoka, she had never liked Hibarigaoka, but here she was, sitting on my chair, drinking sake-laced tea.

"Can you hand me a doughnut?" Linda asked. "Make that two. I hope the boys aren't driving my mother-in-law crazy, but it's her fault if they do. She spoils them rotten." She topped off our cups. I bit into my doughnut. It was lighter than a Dunkin' Donut in America, not as heavy and sweet. It had been a long time since I'd eaten doughnuts. Up until my husband left for India, I ate the calcium rich diet he'd cooked for me. Seaweed three times a day and for snacks, too. Seaweed chopped up with cucumber, which he had served to me with a rice vinegar dressing. Miso soup with seaweed floating in it. Rice balls wrapped with dried seaweed. "I'll turn green if I eat any more seaweed," I had told him. "I'll look like a Martian. I'll stick out even more than I already do."

"At the bonesetter's the other day, a little boy with a broken arm told me what a big nose I had," I said to Linda.

"I wish they wouldn't do that. And didn't I tell you to go to a proper doctor? I would never let anyone yank on my limbs to set them straight."

"He only did that the first time he saw me."

"Still."

"It didn't hurt and even if it did I wasn't going to yell, because none of his Japanese patients yelled, even though I could see they were in pain."

"I would have yelled," Linda said. "I would have yelled my head off. I'm going to scream bloody murder during this labor and Koki will be too embarrassed to ever again show his face in the delivery room. Of course, this is the first time they're letting him in. And the last child we're having." Linda crossed her arms over her stomach, knocking her doughnuts to the floor.

"Don't bend," I said as she started to lean over for them.

"No more sex for him," Linda said. "Hand me another doughnut and turn down the volume on the TV." I turned down the volume on the TV. I took the last doughnut out of the box for Linda. I picked up the doughnuts she had dropped on the floor, lay them in the box, and closed the lid.

"It would be easier if he was in love with her," Kazuko said as the TV announcer pointed to a town in Okinawa where the cherry blossoms were already at their peak. "It would be easier if I knew he couldn't live without her. Then I could be jealous of her. I could hate her. But the note makes me feel sorry for her."

"It wouldn't be easier," Linda said.

On the veranda of the house across the street, a woman in a yellow apron beat dust out of the family futons with a plastic paddle. Before going to bed last night, I'd tried getting Kazuko to eat.

"Did you ever read *The Tale of Genji*?" Kazuko asked. "Prince Genji has so many women that some of them are peripheral to his life. He seldom visits, but when he does, he's unfailingly kind and courtly. He brings them gifts, robes, poems he has written or delicious food to eat. They know they're not his favorite but still they wait, because Genji's entrancing, because he's charm incarnate, because that's what women do. I wasn't going to be one of Genji's peripheral women. I told my husband that. He knew exactly what I meant, or at least I think he did."

"He knows now that you left," Linda said. "He knows you mean business. How did they sprinkle all these doughnuts with the exact same amount of sugar? And in such a pretty pattern, too."

Kazuko fingered the note. She'd never let go of it. But to my surprise, she suddenly handed it to me.

"I can't read it," I said.

"I don't want you to read it. I want you to take it away from me."

I had long been trying to improve my reading skills in Japanese. I read the advertisements on the walls of the Seibu Ikebukuro Line train. Many of the advertisements were for English schools, such as the one I taught at, and some listed the month when new courses were beginning. I could read the Chinese characters, the kanji, for the months of the year. The days of the week. I knew the kanji for man, and woman, and tree, and Japan, and many other things. I looked around for kanji to read during the long hours I spent on the train. I occupied myself in this way. Sometimes I thought of stories I might write, if writing ever came back to me. I'd write about the train passing so close to buildings that I could see right into them. I could see men playing in the mahjong club just past Ooizumi Gakuen Station, hunched over the boards with cigarettes pressed between their lips, moving the black and white pieces. At Shakujikoen, the train passed in front of a dance school, where little girls in leotards twirled in front of a mirror and at the next stop, Nerima, I could see into someone's apartment, which contained a few furnishings, but somehow looked uninhabited. What am I doing here? I often asked myself. Every day was the same.

"He told me she doesn't mean anything to him," Kazuko said. "But he means something to her. I can see it in the note. I can see it so plainly."

The note was written on good quality paper, thick to the touch, with crease lines in it where it had been folded. When Kazuko tapped ash off the end of her cigarette, I slipped the note into the pocket of my jeans. Early in the morning, while the housewives in the neighborhood were outside sweeping their front stoops, I had sent Kazuko on a walk, insisted she get fresh air. From the window I'd watched her pace up and down the narrow street, smoking one cigarette after another. When she came up the stairs she said she was going to be behind on her freelance job, translating the latest Harlequin romance from English into Japanese. She had already translated a dozen of these romances from English into Japanese. It was a good gig, steady work. "But the writing's terrible," she had said. "Drivel." The book she had brought with her to translate lay on the floor next to me. A white woman with golden hair gazed up into the eyes of a dark-haired man, whose head was bent towards her, whose lips were closing in on hers. Kazuko said she had already translated the first page, that it was about what you'd expect.

"I can't forgive him," Kazuko said. "Not so much because he was mean to me, but because he was mean to her."

"I wouldn't feel sorry for her," Linda said.

"But I do." Kazuko got up and walked restlessly around the room, finally stopping in front of a photo I had taken in Nepal and later framed, of spectators sitting in stands set up on a street in Kathmandu to watch the Kumari festival, in which a five year-old girl who was considered a goddess and had been sequestered since birth was paraded through the streets in a carriage. "When she starts menstruating she's considered a mortal," I said.

"Who you talking about?" Linda asked me with her mouth full.

"The little girl in Nepal that they choose as the Kumari," I said. I explained about the festival. "She's considered a goddess until she gets her period. Then they try to arrange a marriage for her, but nobody wants to be married to somebody who was once a goddess, so the Kumaris always end up old maids."

"Fertility ends her Goddess days," Linda said. "That figures. When I first got pregnant, I wanted to have a girl. I wanted to have a girl in the worst way."

I got up off the floor then. It wasn't particularly easy to do. First, I had to roll over onto my knees and then I had to push down hard on the foot of my good leg as I held the bookcase for balance. When I was upright, I put the crutches leaning against the wall under my arms. I held tightly onto the handles. The skin on the palms of my hands had begun peeling off from gripping the crutches. My husband had bandaged my hands, but since he'd left, the bandages had fallen off. Each step, supported on my hands, was raw and painful. I was wearing out. It had been a mistake to send him away.

"Where are you going?" Linda asked.

"For a walk."

"You can't walk. You have a broken leg."

"Ankle."

"Ankle, leg, whichever. It's a lower limb that's essential to locomotion."

"I still walk. I walk on my crutches. I go to the train station every day. I go up that long flight of stairs and I buy my ticket, and then I walk down another flight of stairs to the platform. I go to the English school. I teach, sitting with my leg up on a chair."

"That's why you're in pain," Linda said. "Sit down, for God's sake. Why did Sachio go to India and leave you alone here?"

"I sent him away."

"What do you mean you sent him away?"

"I told him to go. He said he had to stay and take care of me but he was hovering over me all the time, constantly trying to get me to eat more seaweed. He wouldn't stop feeding me seaweed. There's only so much seaweed a Jewish girl from Cleveland can eat."

"My mother-in-law keeps trying to get me to eat fermented beans that look and taste like puke but I don't send her away," Linda said. "You need Sachio's help. What were you thinking?"

"He was taking my splint off every day. He insisted on giving me acupuncture, but he didn't know how to wrap my leg up right before he put the splint back on. The bonesetter noticed and asked me why I was taking the splint off. 'Don't do that,' he told me. 'You need to leave it on to heal.'"

"Why didn't you tell him your husband's an acupuncturist and was trying to help?"

"It didn't feel like help. I told Sachio not to touch my leg anymore. I told him to keep his hands off. I got so mad I threw the bowl of seaweed he gave me on the floor. We had a huge fight. That's why I sent him to India. I told him he had to go or our marriage would be kaput."

"Tell him to come back now," Linda said. "How are you supposed to cook, let alone eat? You can't manage on your own."

"My landlady brings me food," I said.

"I can go out and get more doughnuts," Kazuko said. "I can make miso soup for you."

"I still don't understand why you sent Sachio away," Linda said.

"I sent my husband away, too," Kazuko said. "I never thought that we'd get divorced."

"Neither did I," Linda said.

"You're not getting divorced, are you?" I said to Linda. "You can't be getting divorced." The air smelled of cigarette smoke and underneath that, more sweetly, of doughnuts. We had eaten all of the doughnuts and drunk all of the tea.

"He won't talk to me. I'm so angry and frustrated."

"But I always thought you two talked, unlike Sachio, who punches holes in the wall when we fight."

"When did that happen?"

I could feel the fluid draining down into my ankle. It was a strange feeling, a slow seeping. The bonesetter had told me to elevate my leg as much as I could but it was harder to do now that I was home by myself. At night, when I took off the splint to bathe my leg, I was awed by the swelling of my ankle, by the throbbing pain. In the letters I wrote to Sachio in India, I didn't say how tired I got trying to cook dinner, how badly my good leg ached the longer I stood on it. I didn't say that it was impossible to carry home groceries because I had to keep my hands on my crutches.

I didn't say that the walk to the train station, which had previously taken ten minutes, now took half an hour. I didn't say how tired I felt going up and down all the subway stairs.

"He punched a hole in the wall when I threw my bowl of seaweed on the floor," I said. I squeezed the handles of my crutches, as I did when going up and down stairs. "Doesn't it sound funny, to fight over seaweed? It could be some kind of comedy routine, except he punched the wall right next to my head." I walked into the kitchen. I propped my crutches against the cupboards and leaned against the sink. It was too low. When I washed dishes I had to bend over, and by the time the dishes were all washed my back hurt.

"I looked for women's shelters in the Japanese phone book," I said. The sink needed cleaning. I threw detergent on a sponge and started scrubbing. "Unfortunately I don't read very well and I was too frightened of Sachio to ask him for help." I took a glass from the cupboard and filled it with water. I drank the whole thing down, then left the glass in the sink. "There probably aren't any shelters anyway. There's no room in Tokyo for that kind of thing." If Kazuko and Linda replied, I didn't hear them over the cherry blossom report, the announcer saying something excitedly about the blooming cherry trees. On Saturday nights, before I'd broken my ankle, before he'd gone to India, my husband and I had taught a yoga class in the Aoyama Community Center across the street from Aoyama Cemetery, which was huge and old and full of gravestones and hundreds of cherry trees. In spring, when our yoga students stood at the windows overlooking the cemetery with their heels up on the exercise bar running the length of the room, they saw cotton candy pink blossoms flowing into the distance as far as they could see.

I wiped my hands on a dish towel. I grabbed my crutches and turned around. I walked back into the living room. "I've had enough of the cherry blossom report," I said. "Let's get out of here."

"What if Sachio misses the wall the next time and hits you?" Linda said.

"Let's talk about something else."

"What if he hits you in the face?"

"He can't. He's in India. It's far away."

"Don't be logical. If we were logical, we wouldn't be married to

Japanese. We would have listened to all of those white people in America and their stereotypes about Japanese men. We would have listened to our grandmothers."

"We were in love," I said.

"I still am," Kazuko said. "In my worst moments, I think about going back to him. I think about calling him. I think about writing him a note, like that woman. I think about telling him it was all a mistake."

"What hurts me the most is that Koki was in Texas," Linda said. "The airline sent him to Houston on a company trip and he slept with the blonde he dated before me. He can't tell me why. Or won't. I'm so angry. I'm just so angry." She put her hands on her belly. It had gotten bigger than in her other pregnancies, or maybe I didn't remember just how big she had gotten with her other two. "I'm not speaking to him right now. I've thought of writing him a note, but I don't want to. I think if I did, I would just say sayōnára. I would walk out." She put the teacups we had used on the tray. "Sayōnára. We need different lives."

"We should write our own romance stories," Kazuko said. "Anti-romance stories. Anti-Harlequin romance stories. You can write them in English and I'll translate them into Japanese. I'm tired of hearing about cherry blossoms. I don't want to see cherry blossoms." She turned off the TV. In the sudden cessation of the cherry blossom report, I heard children's voices from the pavement below, accompanied by the clicking metronome of a woman's high heels.

"Let's go for a walk," I said. "Let's go down to the Ochiai River. I used to go almost every evening and watch the black-crowned night heron fish, but I haven't gone once since my accident. If I can't watch the black-crowned night heron fish once more, I don't know what I'll do."

"I'll go," Kazuko said. "I'll go with you."

"What if he misses the wall the next time and hits you?" Linda repeated.

"It's a beautiful bird," I said. "It has a long white feather that streams out from behind its head. It glides down to the river and perches on the bank and stares into the water, waiting for a fish."

"Why are you talking about fishing?" Linda said. "Why are you talking about damn birds and fishes? What if he misses the wall the next time and hits you in the face? Then you'll have a black eye and a broken leg."

"Ankle," I said.

"Oh Christ," Linda said. She swooped up the doughnut box and picked up the tea tray. She walked scowling past me into the kitchen, slow, wide-legged, balancing the teacups on the tray. A cupboard banged in the kitchen. Water rang in the sink. I sat down in her chair. Kazuko leafed through the Harlequin romance, her head bent forward, her hair hiding her face. She spoke excellent English. Impeccable English. She was surely a superior translator, who wanted to translate something better than Harlequin romances. *The Tale of Genji. The Pillow Book.* I slipped the note she had given me out of my pocket as quietly as I had put it in. Kazuko didn't look up. She pretended to read. I unfolded the note. I didn't need to read it. I knew what it said. I had written the same letter to Sachio on the morning of the day he had left for India, after he had placed his slippers neatly by the door. He stepped into his shoes, and though he closed the door and I didn't see this part, I knew he ran down the steps of our apartment house while our neighbor's dog, a Shiba with the intelligent face of a fox stood at the gate of the house across the alley, watching silently with her dark eyes as my husband, holding his suitcase, walked away. He walked past the Imai family's dry cleaning shop on the right, past the field where Japanese white radishes grew and in August filled the air with their sharply bitter fragrance, past the stand where the man with missing teeth grilled and sold chicken on a stick, past the pachinko parlor and its clatter of pinball machines, its clouds of cigarette smoke and noise, past the shop where the tofu maker had been up since three in the morning making tofu. He walked past the housewives sweeping in front of their gates, past a postman on his motorcycle, beginning his morning delivery of mail. He boarded the train for Ikebukuro, or, as is more likely since it was the morning rush hour, was half-pushed into the train by the line of office workers barreling forward. By then, I was halfway through the letter, and he was being further pushed inside the train by a Seibu Ikebukuro train line employee whose job it was to stand on the platform during the morning rush hour, pressing on the people closest to the door with white-gloved hands as you would press on your clothes to make more room in your suitcase. I hadn't seen him since.

I tore the note in little pieces. I let them slip from my fingers. The note I'd written to Sachio lay folded in a box. Kazuko's eyes were full of pain. From down the street, the piano player was now playing the D minor scale. I walked out onto the veranda, setting my crutches down carefully over the ridge between the door and concrete veranda floor so I wouldn't trip. I held the railing and listened to the D minor scale, cleanly and quickly played. All by itself, the scale was beautiful. I had never before considered the beauty of the D minor scale. I had liked living in Hibarigaoka. I had liked living in a place where neighbors practiced piano, and where I could hang out at dusk with old men from the neighborhood, whose names I didn't know, but who were birdwatchers like me. I had liked living in Japan, where the blooming of cherry trees made the national news. I would mail the note I had written, and Sachio would read it and return to me. I wondered what I'd do before he came. Soon, the cherry trees would bloom in Tokyo. If my ankle was healed, I'd go to see them. I wouldn't have to use crutches. I'd walk down the tree-lined paths of Aoyama Cemetery and stand beneath the blossoming cherry trees.

Crows

First thing in the evening, not long after I had fought my way off a crowded rush hour train, my English student, Mr. Kikuchi, who was an electrical engineer at the University of Tokyo and a smart if usually quiet man, told me that he had put sensors on twenty crows and was tracking their movements night and day.

"Most crows stay in their wooping place," Mr. Kikuchi said. "A few go to Arakawa ward, maybe to eat temple rice. But one crow goes to Roppongi. All the way. Five kilometers there and back. A total of ten. This is a special crow." I stared blankly at Mr. Kikuchi. I adjusted my glasses, which had gotten knocked askew in the crowded train. Through the lens, spotted by smog, I looked at my student, a solemn man from whom, up to now, I had rarely heard a peep. He looked back at me expectantly. My feet had been stepped on. I wanted to take off my shoes and wriggle my toes. I moved to the side of the doorway, and Mr. Kikuchi followed, his black eyes fixed on my face. The other students poured into the classroom, opened briefcases, and took out textbooks and dictionaries and pens. They worked at places like Daiichi Kangyo Bank, or Yomiuri Securities, or the Tokyo Stock Exchange. They were dressed in black, like mourners at a funeral, or like crows.

"Excuse me Mr. Kikuchi," I said. I hesitated. What had he just said to me? I didn't want to ask him, because then he'd know he hadn't said it right. I hated correcting my students' English. They expected to be corrected. They wanted to be corrected. Their whole lives, they had been corrected. "Mr. Kikuchi, what is a wooping place?" Mr. Kikuchi swiveled on his heel and pointed to his seat in the third row of the classroom. "That's my wooping place," he said and turned and pointed at my desk, "and that's yours." His eyes were alive with intelligence, and something else I'd never seen in class. Excitement. I was a bad English teacher. A boring English teacher. Mr. Kikuchi was excited about crows. "I don't understand," I said. I wanted to add that I had been up since 5:30 that morning, when I gobbled down rice and ran for the train. I had already taught three English classes at two different locations, and was facing this, my last and longest class of the day, in a state of exhaustion and ennui. I wanted to tell Mr. Kikuchi that I was too tired to continue the noble struggle to understand Japanese-English. I wanted to speak Japanese, but I was supposed to be teaching English, so English I spoke.

"Mr. Kikuchi, I'm sorry. I'm not following you. I don't understand what you're trying to say."

Mr. Kikuchi turned and pointed at Mr. Hara, a middle-aged salaryman with hair like Albert Einstein's, though slightly shorter, and a forehead just as vast. Though our textbook, *English for All*, sat open before him on his desk, Mr. Hara appeared to be asleep. And who wouldn't be, with a three hour commute each day? Add to that a nine hour workday and then a three hour English class and you had a man half-dead with fatigue. I couldn't look at him and complain about my day.

"This," Mr. Kikuchi said, walking over to Mr. Hara, "is Mr. Hara's wooping place." He rapped on Mr. Hara's chair with his pen and Mr. Hara awakened from his slumbers and said succinctly, and in English, "What is wooping place?" He looked pleased about his clear English sentence, and there was an immediate response, a rustle in the classroom, and then a rapid, quick-fire low-burning conversation began in Japanese. Everyone opened their dictionaries. Index fingers moved from the top to the bottom of pages. Even Mr. Hara, now wide awake, searched from the top to the bottom of his page.

"Woost," Miss Tanaka said. She worked as an OL, an office lady, at Daiichi Kangyo Bank and was always the first student out of the gate. "Birds woost," she said. "Sit on nest."

"Yes, woops," Mr. Kikuchi said.

"No, Kikuchi-san," Miss Tanaka said. "You have to concentrate and pronunciate correctly. 'Woost. R-o-o-s-t.' Say it."

"Woost."

"Better."

"This is Hara-san's woosting place," Mr. Kikuchi said.

"You are incorrect," Miss Tanaka said. "Hara-san's study place is Tokyo YMCA College of English, but woosting place is Chiba. Ne, Hara-san, isn't it?"

"It is. I and my wife and son live there. Also my mother and father. All in a small nest."

"Oh!" I exclaimed. "You're talking about roosting, right? Birds roosting? Making nests?"

"Exactly!" Mr. Kikuchi said. "Crows woost in Ueno Park. They eat garbage left by humans, and food of zoo animals, too. I put sensors on crows. I track their movements, where they go."

"Why?" Miss Tanaka asked.

"Because government command me. There is crow problem in Tokyo. Big crow problem."

"Big crows, too," Mr. Hara said. "My neighbor in Chiba, he get attacked by big crow. Crow dive at him like airplane. Wife is afraid to go out of house. Daughter is afraid to come over. Mailman is afraid to leave mail."

"Kyaa, kyaa, kyaa!" Mr. Kikuchi uttered in a harsh, deep voice. "Kyaa, kyaa, kyaa!" Miss Tanaka dropped her dictionary. I froze in the act of taking off my coat. Mr. Hara, looking wide-eyed at Mr. Kikuchi, looked as wide awake as he had ever been.

"Segoi, Kikuchi-san, karasu ni sokkuri nitte iru ne," Miss Tanaka said, and the other students all began speaking excitedly in Japanese.

"Does crow sound like that?" Mr. Kikuchi asked in his usual quiet voice. He bounded across the room, and pounced on Miss Tanaka's dictionary. She blushed and looked flustered.

"Yes!" Mr. Hara said. "Exactly! That is the voice of my neighbor's crow!"

"Then he is jungle crow." Mr. Kikuchi ran to the blackboard with Miss Tanaka's dictionary, picked up a piece of chalk, and began to draw with sweeping strokes. "Jungle crow has thick beak curved like this. He is fierce crow if nest is attacked." He drew eyes, feathers, a tail, clawed feet. The crow was enormous. It filled up the blackboard. I could almost hear the beat of its large wings. An image of Mr. Kikuchi as a man-sized crow flying across Ueno Park appeared before me, with the rest of the class, led by Miss Tanaka, flying behind him. I'd always wanted to fly. Sometimes I'd flown in my dreams. But I'd never wanted to be a crow.

"Why crow attack neighbor?" Mr. Hara asked. "Kikuchi-san, do you know?"

"Because neighbor is too near nest. Crow dislikes this, especially if nest contain baby crows."

"What should neighbor do?" Mr. Hara asked.

"He should get a cat," Miss Tanaka said.

"He has a cat," Mr. Hara said. "It is–Eigo de nan to ya no ka na? Fraidy cat. Because crow is so big. Too big. It is monster crow."

"This is fault of Tokyo people," Mr. Kikuchi said. "They make too many garbage. Crows like to eat it. Then they become big crows."

"Too much garbage," Miss Tanaka said. "Not too many."

"Yes. Too much people make too much garbage," Mr. Kikuchi said.

"Then crows become like Piggy Pans," Mr. Hara said. Everyone thought about this for a moment.

"Like what?" I finally asked.

"Piggy Pans. Boy who is Charlie Brown's friend."

"Pigpen? You mean Pigpen? I can't imagine Pigpen in Japan. Everything here is so clean."

"Pigpen, yes, Pigpen!" Mr. Hara said. "I mix up Pigpen with Peter Pans. Peter Pans is clean and can fly, and everyone loves him too much. Pigpen is dusty. People always say, 'Take a bath, take a bath.' But he never take a bath. He doesn't like to be clean."

"Who is this Piggy?" Miss Tanaka said. "He doesn't sound nice. He sounds dirty, like crows."

"Crows are not dirty," Mr. Kikuchi said.

"I like Pigpen very much, but Charlie Brown is a good man, too. Charlie Brown wants to kick a football, but every time, Lucy takes it away." Mr. Hara sprang out of his chair and leaned over with his hand out, holding an imaginary football by its tip. He gave it a kick and then straightened up and beamed. He was obviously fond of comic books, as were all the Japanese. If only *English for All* were a comic book, it might then be fun to read. According to the introduction in the teacher's manual, it was a "linguistic text of intermediate to advanced complexity, designed to be modeled by the teacher for the students, who should then model it for each other and transfer their practice to the real world stage." If only the teacher's manual were a comic book.

Miss Tanaka reached for the dictionary that always lay on her desk in plain view, but her hand closed on empty space and she appeared to be at a loss for words. Whenever she was at a loss for words she found one in her dictionary, but Mr. Kikuchi still had it. He said, "This Pigpen may be dirty. But crows are not."

"Crows love to eat garbage," Miss Tanaka said. She eyed her dictionary longingly. "You said so yourself, Kikuchi-san."

"You don't understand." Mr. Kikuchi carefully placed his chalk in the chalk tray and paced at the front of the room. "How can I explain? It is difficult to say. Not easy."

"It is easy," Miss Tanaka said. "You love crows."

"I'm a scientist. We don't talk about love or not love."

"Why not?" Miss Tanaka looked Mr. Kikuchi in the eye. He didn't look away. I had been warned not to look anyone in the eye for longer than sixty seconds by none other than Elsie and Fumiko, whose *Japan Times* column on Japanese etiquette was read by every foreign woman living in Japan that I knew. The lack of eye contact from the Japanese drove English teachers crazy the first six months they taught here. You looked at the students when you asked a question. They didn't look in your eyes when they answered, but somewhere down below, at your chin or nose. Miss Tanaka still had Mr. Kikuchi impaled in her gaze. Surely sixty seconds had passed. Who had come up with this number? Perhaps a scientist such as Mr. Kikuchi had wandered the streets of Tokyo with a stopwatch, timing the eye contact, or lack thereof, between the Japanese. Whoever he was, he had not timed Miss Tanaka and Mr. Kikuchi. How long were they going to stare at each other without saying a word?

"Crows eat garbage," Miss Tanaka said. "You said so yourself."

"They eat, because it is easy food for them to catch. But who makes this garbage? We Japanese say we love nature. But everywhere, we drop garbage. For every thousand people in Tokyo, there is one crow. If there are one people for every thousand crows, Japan would be very clean place. But it is not, because we throw everything away. When shoes become one year old, we buy new ones. We use chopsticks one time, then throw them away. Chopsticks become garbage. New shoes become garbage. Whole of Japan is becoming garbage. One day, from the stars, star people will look at Japan, but they won't see anything nice. They won't see blue sky and green forest. They won't see top of Mt. Fuji and certainly not bottom. They'll just see garbage." Miss Tanaka's dictionary slid out of Mr. Kikuchi's grasp and fell with a slam onto the floor. Miss Tanaka flinched. Mr. Hara jumped backwards, almost knocking over his chair.

"Mr. Kikuchi, please give me my dictionary," Miss Tanaka said.

"I will not," Mr. Kikuchi said.

I gasped. Miss Tanaka didn't. Mr. Hara, looking as stunned as Charlie Brown looked when his foot met air instead of the football, sat down hard in his chair. Mr. Kikuchi picked up Miss Tanaka's dictionary. I opened my mouth to tell him to give it back to her. Instead, what came out was, "I want to see your Ueno Park crows."

"You do?" Mr. Kikuchi said.

"Crows are everywhere," Miss Tanaka said. "You don't need going to Ueno Park to see crows."

"I know they're everywhere, but I've never paid attention to them." I had stopped paying attention to everything, I had become numb to all views. It had taken me four weeks to learn my students' names this term when it usually took me only two. They dressed alike, looked alike, acted alike, or so I had assumed. I no longer saw the housewives on the street, riding their child-sized bicycles, or the shopkeepers who greeted me cheerfully, who sold me fish or tofu or udon noodles or bean sweets. I no longer saw the old women hunched over in the rice fields, and the salarymen, their sons and grandsons, endless numbers of them riding blank-faced on the train. I never saw my husband, who was always at work. Though I'd once enjoyed looking at the Tokyo YMCA College of English building, which had been designed by a Tokyo architectural firm to look like a melting ice cube held up by sticks, I now only rushed through the door.

"I want to see crows, too," Mr. Hara declared.

"Who asked you?" Miss Tanaka said.

"When do you want to go?" Mr. Kikuchi asked.

"How about now?" Mr. Hara said.

"Now we are supposed to have English lesson," Miss Tanaka said.

"We don't need classroom to have English lesson," Mr. Hara said. "We only need English speaker. Native English speaker. We don't need desk and chairs."

"I need. I need desk and chair and especially dictionary. I cannot have English lesson without it."

"Why?" Mr. Hara asked.

"It is impossible."

"Always, human being has to try new way. You can try English lesson in Ueno Park, with grass and trees."

"Mr. Toda will forbid us to leave. He won't permit," Miss Tanaka said. Mr. Toda was the director of the Tokyo YMCA College of English. He was a large man who liked to walk the hallways and scare his teachers by lumbering unannounced into their classrooms. Even if we managed to slip away unnoticed, all fifteen of us, what would he say when he walked into an empty room?

"We won't ask Mr. Toda," Mr. Hara said. "We'll go by own steam."

"Mr. Toda will see us leave," Miss Tanaka said. "He has eyes behind head. Front, too."

"If Mr. Toda sees us, Kikuchi-san can give his crow-cry. It will scare Mr. Toda very much. He'll run away."

"I don't think so," Miss Tanaka said.

I almost laughed at the thought of Mr. Toda, bear-like and balding and middle- aged, fleeing at the cry of a crow, but then I was middle-aged too, or nearly so.

"I have an idea!" Mr. Hara exclaimed. He plunged both hands into the large bag beside his chair and tossed out a smashed rice ball and several comic books before withdrawing a rope, thickly braided, turquoise and yellow and white, coil upon coil of it. He carried the rope to the front of the room. He tied one end of it around the fat iron legs of my desk and then walked to the windows at the back of the room. He opened one window with a grunt, and then another. He stuck his head out the window. He drew it back into the room.

"Mr. Hara? What are you doing?" I said.

Mr. Hara held the remaining coils of rope out the window and let go. He stuck one leg out, too.

"Mr. Hara!"

"I'm going to Ueno Park," Mr. Hara announced cheerfully. He disappeared from view.

Everyone rushed to the windows. Below us, halfway to the street, we saw Mr. Hara clinging to the side of the building, Spiderman in a suit, grinning up at us and looking very much at ease. He let go of the rope with one hand, and waved. He called out comments on the temperature and view.

"Don't move!" I shouted, so loudly that two salarymen, walking side-by-side in the street below, stopped to point at Mr. Hara and then at me. It was not polite to point in Japan. It was not polite to touch anyone on the head. The head was the seat of intelligence, the repository of the soul. I wanted to drop something out of the window to get Mr. Hara's attention, but what if it hit him on the head? Mr. Hara waved to his admirers. "Nice weather," he called out in Japanese. I leaned out the window and was about to let out another yell when my Ohio State University class ring slid off my sweaty finger and whizzed towards Mr. Hara. He grabbed for it and missed. His feet, for a moment, left their perch. Miss Tanaka screamed. The ring plummeted to the ground. A feathered black torpedo cawed "Ha! Ha! Ha!" and snatched it up, then perched on a neon sign. A crow. A crow with a fondness for rings, attracted by the sparkle of the stone. A crow with glossy blue-back wings. A crow with a class ring, which I had to retrieve. There was no other choice. Once I'd wanted to be an overseas reporter. Now I was a thirty-five year old gaijin, teaching English to the Japanese. Soon I wouldn't be able to do anything other than teach English to the Japanese. That's all I'd been doing for the past seven years.

I tore off my coat. I turned around and stuck one leg out the window. The architects who had designed the Tokyo YMCA College of English had covered the building with reinforced concrete grids which looked like the paper Japanese children practiced writing their Chinese characters on, one small square after another, punctuated by aluminum rods which looked like sticks and stood up straight, like the hair of somebody who was getting an electric shock. I wondered if the grids would hold the weight of a woman who was scared out of her wits. I took a deep breath, grabbed the rope, and felt for the lip of the first grid. I gripped the sill and tentatively lowered my weight onto it. I lifted my other leg out the window. Miss Tanaka reached for me, but I was out of reach, I was going down, and then I could hear nothing but the blood rushing through my ears. A Yurakucho line train ran by, deep within the earth. I felt the vibration, the trembling, the speed. I felt the buildings crowding in, and then I heard Mr. Hara say, put your foot here, and here, and here. Don't look down. How precisely he gave instructions in English. Where had he learned to? Not from *English for All* and not from me. I gripped the rope. I pressed my cheek to the concrete. I placed my feet as precisely as a tightrope walker. "Let go," Mr. Hara said. "You're on the earth. Let go."

I let go of the rope. The fragrance of cherry blossoms filled the air, silken petals swept by on the breeze. Like the Japanese, I was always working. I had not noticed it was spring.

"Teacher, are you okay?" Miss Tanaka called down.

"I'm fine," I said, feeling immensely happier. "I'm great!"

"You climb very well," Mr. Hara said. "Have you done it before?"

I burst out laughing, I bent over laughing. I laughed until tears ran down my cheeks. "No," I said when I could speak. "Mr. Hara, do you always carry a rope around the city?"

"I'm rock climber. At least, before marriage, I'm rock climber. My wife, she doesn't like me to do climbing now. She says if I fall she has to raise children alone. Actually, one child and two old parents. But still, I sometimes train for climbing. It was easy climb, don't you think?"

"Teacher?" Miss Tanaka called from the window. "Mr. Toda is coming down the hall. What should we do?"

I was going to lose my job because of a crow. The crow dipped its head and peered at me. It walked with a strut along the top of the neon sign, my ring in its beak.

"Teacher?" Miss Tanaka looked at me like I would know what to do. Students always expected you to know what to do.

"Sit down in your seat," I said.

"But I don't want to sit down, I want to join you." One stocking clad leg emerged from the window of our second floor room.

"Don't! If you want to come outside, go out the door! Please! All of you!"

"I can't go out the door, Mr. Toda is coming in. I think he heard me scream." Then Miss Tanaka was out the window, holding for dear life onto the rope. She began to descend, stepping, as I had done, on the lip of each grid. When she had gone one story down, Mr. Toda's large head popped into view. He stared at Miss Tanaka, and then at Mr. Hara, and finally at me. In a booming voice he shouted, "Mrs. Rosenboo? What are you doing? What are you doing?"

Miss Tanaka froze. Her hands turned white on the rope. "Mr. Hara," I said softly so that Miss Tanaka couldn't hear. "Miss Tanaka is in trouble."

"It's okay," Mr. Hara said. "She's not in trouble. I'll talk to Mr. Toda. I'll explain." Before I could say that she had lost her nerve, Mr. Hara called up to Mr. Toda, using respect language, speaking calmly in the politest Japanese. I moved right up to the wall, under Miss Tanaka. Mr. Hara's two admirers, the salarymen who had stopped to chat with him while he was on his rope, stepped up to the wall with me, too. Perhaps we could catch Miss Tanaka if she fell. Don't let her fall, I prayed. Let me lose my job. But let Miss Tanaka grow wings.

"Miss Tanaka?" I tried to still the tremor in my voice. "Are you okay?"

"No," Miss Tanaka said. The Japanese mixed up yes and no in English. They mixed up him and her. I hoped that Miss Tanaka meant yes when she said no.

"Don't let go of the rope," I said. "There's another grid below you. You can reach it with your foot."

"Grid? What is grid?"

"Ledge."

"I don't know this word. I need my dictionary," Miss Tanaka said hotly. She seemed to unfreeze. She slid her left hand a little ways down the rope. Mr. Toda's voice rose. After one glance at Mr. Kikuchi, who was leaning out the window watching Miss Tanaka with a worried look on his face, I concentrated on Miss Tanaka, I tried to speak as calmly to her as Mr. Hara was to Mr. Toda, I tried to tune out the sounds of beeping horns and the murmuring of Mr. Hara's admirers and Mr. Toda's loud voice.

"A ledge is a piece of the building that sticks out," I said. "This building has them all over. They're about the width of your foot."

"I don't know ledge. I don't know ledge, because of Mr. Kikuchi, that thief."

"Listen to me. A ledge is a piece of the building that sticks out. Like the branch of a tree. It's below you. Just a little ways. Put your foot on it." I repeated this several times, until one of Miss Tanaka's feet left its perch. I held my breath. Her foot swung in the air, then found the lip of the grid. She let her weight down. She said, "Mr. Kikuchi stole my dictionary."

"I know. You'll get it back. Keep going. Miss Tanaka? Another step down. One more to go." I reached for her. Miss Tanaka grabbed my hand and let go of the rope. "Mr. Kikuchi is a very rude man," she said. "Not typical Japanese." She brushed herself off. "I don't know ledge. I don't know grid. I want my dictionary."

"I've always wanted to travel around the world," I blurted out.

"Me too. That's why I study English all the time. Mr. Toda is angry at you."

Mr. Toda was shouting at me in Japanese. I pretended not to understand a word. This was a tried and true gaijin tactic which always worked. It shouldn't work in my case, because I could speak Japanese. Although Mr. Toda was the administrator of a language school and, presumably, believed that a foreign language could be learned, he still didn't believe I could speak Japanese, because it was an impossibly difficult language. He had told me that he was pleased he ran a school where English was taught instead of Japanese. Everyone could learn English, but few, he had informed me, could learn Japanese.

"Mr. Toda says he will come down here," Miss Tanaka said.

"He is too big to use rope," Mr. Hara said.

"He can go out the door," Miss Tanaka said.

"That's true," Mr. Hara said. "But I think he will stay at window and continue shouting from there. He is big man. Big man likes shouting. He enjoys too much to stop. As human being, this is Mr. Toda's weak point. Now Mr. Kikuchi is telling him, teacher forgot coat. And Miss Tanaka forgot dictionary."

"I didn't forget," Miss Tanaka said. "Mr. Kikuchi stole it from me."

"Kikuchi-san is saying he will come down here. And Mr. Toda is saying, no, stay here. But Kikuchi-san is good customer. Also, he is big scientist at Todai. Todai is famous university. So Mr. Toda is nice to him. Mr. Toda is saying, 'Don't leave.' To teacher, he says 'Go.' But to Kikuchi-san, he says, 'Stay here.' Teacher, I got big trouble for class and especially you. Lucy says Charlie Brown is blockhead. I am too."

"I like Charlie Brown."

"You do? Me too!"

"Kikuchi-san can climb very well," Miss Tanaka said. "But he should use two hands on the rope."

Something plummeted from the sky and slammed onto the concrete. I stared, horrified, at the place where it fell, and then sank to my knees in relief when I saw that it was *Kodansha's Unabridged English-Japanese*. I was about to pick it up when Mr. Kikuchi landed lightly beside it and snatched it from beneath my nose. I jumped to my feet. The crow, still holding my class ring, took wing. It rose into the sooty skies of Tokyo, towards the tarnished brass globe of the sun. Aghast, I watched it leave.

"That crow is one of my crows!" Mr. Kikuchi said.

"How can you tell?" Miss Tanaka said. "All crows look alike to me."

"Crow is holding something in beak," Mr. Hara said. "Must be tasty bite to eat."

"It's not," Miss Tanaka said. "It's a wedding ring."

"Are you married?" Mr. Kikuchi said.

"Yes," Miss Tanaka said. "I mean no." But Mr. Kikuchi had already taken off down the street in the direction the crow, now a black speck, had flown. "Give me back my dictionary!" Miss Tanaka cried out and took off after him, moving surprisingly quickly despite being clad in a skirt and heels. "Teacher, we have to go too," Mr. Hara said. The rest of my students looked down at me beseechingly from the windows. I wanted to call to them to go out the door, to walk out of the classroom and down the hall and down the stairs. The rope dangled below them, Rapunzel's hair. I knew they weren't going to move. Mr. Hara followed my gaze. "They're okay," he said. But how did he know that was true? I was surrounded by the gray buildings of Kanda. They hid the spring sky from view, they blocked the breeze. Dark-suited working men and women were heading to the bars to drink, or to the Kanda train station for home. They'd eat, wait for their turn to soak in the bath, lay out their futons for sleep. The next morning it would all begin again, the constant rush to go somewhere, nowhere, to never move. I had to move.

The front door of the college burst open and Mr. Toda, scowling and huge, was suddenly breathing in my face. Mr. Hara began to apologize profusely for his endangerment of life and limb, though I couldn't seem to make out his exact words, only fragments here and there, like the glimpses of my neighborhood, seen in the days when I could see. I remembered the cluster of stores that hugged the sides of the main street, the pottery shop filled with colored ware, the hardware store where I'd purchased the broom I used, and the tofu maker, unusually tall for a Japanese, as tall as me, wearing his wide white apron, smiling his wide smile at me. At the vegetable shop the clerk who had later died of drink thumped a pumpkin on its orange belly and exclaimed "Listen! Listen to the sound!" I saw Mr. Kikuchi running back towards me. Leave, I wanted to tell him, but the word wouldn't come out, either in English or Japanese. It was a whisper in my mind, soon gone like the cherry blossom petals on the breeze, like the crow on the wing. I tried to speak louder but couldn't seem to get enough air to support the words, and my students at the window of the building, Mr. Ishi, whose name meant stone though he was not like a stone in the least, and Miss Kano and Mr. Kawabata and all the others looked down at me. They began to apologize. Everyone except Mr. Toda was apologizing. Mr. Hara's two admirers, the salarymen who had been watching, were backing away, bowing in apology, apologizing for watching. Then they turned and fled. Mr. Hara was apologizing for his rope. My students were leaning out the window, apologizing to the air.

"Gomen nasái," Miss Kano mouthed the words. "Senséi, gomen nasái."

Japanese women speak softly, Elsie and Fumiko had said in a column I'd read years ago. *You don't have to speak that softly, but it would be wise to modulate your voice.*

"Gomen nasái," Miss Kano whispered to me.

"Sit down in your seat!" Mr. Toda yelled. Miss Kano gaped at me and then she was gone. They were all gone and the rope was being pulled up, I couldn't see by whom. Its colorful tail gave one last swish at the grids of the building, at the melting curved walls, and then disappeared. I knew my students were taking their seats. Mr. Toda had made them sit down. I had not been able to make Miss Tanaka sit down. Perhaps that was a good thing.

"Teacher? Teacher?" It was Mr. Kikuchi, saying between gasps for air that he had not been able to catch the crow which took Miss Tanaka's ring.

"Teacher? Teacher?" It was Miss Tanaka now, as breathless as Mr. Kikuchi, as urgent in her appeal. But I was no longer their teacher.

"Mrs. Rosenboo? Mrs. Rosenboo?" Mr. Toda threw open *English for All.* "You're fired," he read from dialogue 14A. He flipped through several pages. "No severance pay!" He stepped closer. I backed away.

"Mr. Toda, you are a very rude man!" Miss Tanaka said. "Not typical Japanese."

Mr. Toda looked stunned. He didn't say a word.

"Teacher!" Miss Tanaka said commandingly. "Follow me!"

We turned, all four of us at once, and ran down Kando dori. I had never run down Kando dori. The Tokyo pace was a fast walk, a clipped walk, in which eye contact was seldom made, even when you stepped on someone's foot. "Tanaka-san is like Lucy," Mr. Hara said as we flashed past surprised lovers with dyed yellow hair standing up straight on their heads like a cock's crest. A couple sitting in front of slices of kiwi cake in a coffee shop window stared. We ran past salarymen hurrying to the station, past staggering drunks, past smokers puffing smoke into the air. We ran past blue-suited schoolchildren clutching black book bags, past white-gloved taxi drivers who leaned out of their windows to stare. We ran past a gauntlet of shops with their goods spilling into the street, TV's, calculators, cameras instant and otherwise, handmade papers of every hue, stationery of all kinds, envelopes adorned with gold and silver bows, Japanese dolls dressed in silk kimonos, and the food, perfect life-like models of it encased under glass, noodles suspended from lacquered chopsticks, tuna sushi, plump and red on its nest of rice, okonomiyaki in a flat perfect circle, looking more real than the real thing. The sun was just beginning to set. The neon lights above us threw glittering colors at our feet. Flags and banners waved overhead, advertising slip-pers, English classes, sex tours to Thailand, pachinko parlors, porno shops, video games, "creative" love hotels, caskets, kimono shops, cram schools, comic books, a shop where you could buy designer clothes and drink tea, cafes, Western beds with canopies over them, special neckties with Japanese haiku embroidered on them in gold thread, McDonald's hamburgers, Buddhist altars, kites, Japanese sweets, electronic goods of every kind. Everything was for sale, everything could be bought and sold and then, as Mr. Kikuchi had said, thrown away. I had thrown away my life. I was running out of air.

"Lucy is fussbudget," Mr. Hara said over our pounding feet. "Fussbudget is sometimes good leader. This fussbudget can run very well. She is brave, too." We followed Miss Tanaka up the Kanda train station stairs. She came to a halt at the end of the long line in front of the ticket machine and dabbed sweat off her face with a neatly folded handkerchief. My breath tore ragged in my throat. I was out of shape, although I walked miles underground, in the subterranean tunnels of the subway, where I was often mistaken, from behind, for a Japanese. People asked me directions and when I turned around to give them, they exclaimed, "It's a foreigner!" and then asked somebody else.

"Mr. Hara, did you say something about me?" Miss Tanaka asked.

"You were very brave against Mr. Toda," Mr. Hara said. He was not out of breath in the least. "You were like Lucy. Lucy always speaks her mind. Lucy always says direct things to Charlie Brown and everyone else. It was sugoi. It was brave way."

"But it doesn't matter. I said these things to Mr. Toda. Then I leave. Left. I left behind *English for All*. My dictionary is gone. I threw away my dream."

"I will give you my *English for All*," Mr. Hara said.

"Why bother?" I said. "Nobody in that book has anything interesting to say. Today we've been talking about crows, but nobody in *English for All* talks about crows, because there are no crows in *English for All*. There are no Joe Manginis or Herbert Arnovitzes or Betsy Birnbaums, the kids I grew up with in Cleveland, and there are no Lakshmi Guptas, who was the best fisherman in Girl Scout camp in the sixth grade. There are no fish in *English for All*. No rivers or mountains or trees. There's only Mr. Smith and Mr. Brown and Mr. Nelson, who have boring jobs and boring and meaningless conversations about nothing. *English for All* should be titled *English for None, Doing Nothing*. Good riddance to that book! I never want to read it again."

"I like *English for All*," Miss Tanaka said.

"Why?" I snapped, but then saw how distressed she looked. I realized that I had been shouting in her face. The woman in line ahead of us was giving me a look, and Mr. Hara's eyebrows had risen so high up his forehead they were about to disappear into his hair. "You can get a new *English for All*," I said in a quieter voice.

"Yes, I can get books, but I cannot go back to Tokyo YMCA College of English. My company is sponsoring my English classes. They are paying fee. Now I cannot go back. I burned up my bridge."

"You can study somewhere else," I said, but Miss Tanaka didn't look reassured in the least. "There are hundreds of English schools in Tokyo."

"My company president is friends with Mr. Toda. They have long-time association. Every person from my company studies English at this school. I cannot explain to my president. Never. Maybe I will lose my job, because Mr. Toda will give a bad report about me. I will lose opportunity. I cannot speak more about these things."

"What opportunity?" I asked.

"To go to Sydney office. They never sent a woman to the Sydney office before. They always sent a man. But I had a chance to go, if I study English hard. Now I don't."

"I'll go back to the college," I said. "I'll talk to Mr. Toda."

"I will, too," Mr. Hara said.

"Me, too," Mr. Kikuchi said. "I'll explain."

"Please don't," Miss Tanaka said. Her eyes glittered with tears. "We cannot go back," she said. She turned away from us and faced the ticket machine. My eyes filled with tears, too. What could I do? It would be impossible for me to apologize to Mr. Toda, impossible to make amends. I'd burned my bridges, too.

"I'm sorry about your dictionary," Mr. Kikuchi blurted out. "I don't mean bad things. Please take it back."

"No," Miss Tanaka said. "You can keep."

"I'm sorry about your ring, too," Mr. Kikuchi said. "At Ueno Park, we can track crow who took it by computer. Crow has sensor attached to it. Maybe we can get back your ring."

I opened my mouth to say that the ring wasn't Miss Tanaka's, that it was mine, but before I could say a word Miss Tanaka said, "Doesn't matter. Crow can keep."

"I think you care more about English class than wedding ring," Mr.

Kikuchi said. "I think you care more about dictionary than wedding ring. Maybe you should leave your husband and come with me."

The back of Miss Tanaka's neck turned red. Sounds came out of Mr. Hara's mouth, but none of them formed words. Mr. Kikuchi held Miss Tanaka's dictionary to his breast. A smile hovered at his lips. The Japanese were notoriously shy. Everyone knew this, especially the Japanese. I had had to fling my arms around my husband, then only a handsome stranger I'd met by chance under icy stars in Nepal at fifteen thousand feet. The man had seemed frozen himself. Three hugs before he melted and we rendezvoused in my tent, four rendezvous and he had proposed. Mr. Kikuchi was not at all like I had thought. Perhaps none of the Japanese were like I had thought. The smell of yakitori chicken wafted to my nose, the ground trembled beneath my feet. For a moment I thought it was an earthquake, but then I realized it was a train coming in. When the latest earthquake had struck Tokyo, I had been in the British library in Iidabashi, searching the stacks for books. As the earth began to shake, the Japanese had stood there calmly holding up the bookcases until the tremors ceased. After this event, nobody had looked anybody else in the eye. No sympathetic glances had been exchanged, no proposals or propositions made, no hugs imposed or exchanged. Everyone had simply resumed reading their books. But perhaps, under imperturbable exteriors, the Japanese were thinking about crows, or about climbing out of buildings by rope, or proposing under foreign stars to foreign lovers at fifteeen thousand feet. The line moved forward. Miss Tanaka stepped forward, too, then stopped and turned around. Her face was so red I thought she must be red down to her toes, but her voice, when it came out, was as steady and polite as the gaze she trained on Mr. Kikuchi's face.

"Mr. Kikuchi? I'll take back my dictionary now. I'm going home."

"I think Mr. Kikuchi likes your dictionary too much to give it back," Mr. Hara said. "Kikuchi-san, isn't that so?"

"No," Mr. Kikuchi said.

"Mr. Kikuchi?" I said. "Give Miss Tanaka's dictionary back to her."

"I'll only give it back after she sees crows."

"I'm not interested in crows," Miss Tanaka said. "Everyone is not interested in same things."

"At first I didn't care about crows either. But when I put a sensor on them I got to see them closely. I got to pick them up. They have fine feathers. They are good birds. Please come. Please."

"Okay, I'll go," Miss Tanaka said angrily. "I can't return home without my dictionary. I have no choice."

We reached the front of the line. Miss Tanaka dropped coins into the ticket machine. She handed us our tickets and said, "Follow me." She walked briskly towards the line in front of the ticket punchers. The ticket punchers punched our tickets and she charged up the station stairs with Mr. Hara at her heels.

"Miss Tanaka isn't married," I said to Mr. Kikuchi as we hurried along after them.

"I know. She is Miss. Miss Crow." He looked up and down the platform. "Where did she go? There! Hurry please." A train was pulling in. We stepped into the line that Miss Tanaka and Mr. Hara were standing in and filed aboard. The train was so packed I couldn't even turn my head, but Miss Tanaka stood directly in my line of vision. Her face was stony. One hand lay clenched in a fist against the side of her purse. She had never mentioned she wanted to go abroad. She had never mentioned she wanted to leave. She was perhaps twenty-eight years old. I tutored a private student, also twenty-eight years old, who had been complaining to me that her boss was trying to push her out of her job. He kept hinting that he expected her to be having a baby soon, that she was at that age when women left their companies and stayed at home, and why wasn't she?

The train stopped. The doors opened. A crowd of people got off but an even bigger crowd got on, revelers on their way to the park. The train lurched on its way, rumbled rapidly over the tracks and then stopped. Ueno Station. I was carried along in the crush by the festive throng that poured out of the train and flowed down the station stairs. Everywhere, as far as the eye could see, the cherry trees were in bloom. Pink blossoms, white blossoms, snow flowers blooming on the trees. The odor of yakitori chicken, of rice balls and seaweed, of beer being guzzled filled the air. Light bulbs flashed everywhere, men and women posed with their arms around each other, snatches of conversation came to my ears. Lanterns had been hung from the trees. An elephant trumpeted from Ueno Park zoo. The crowd bore me along, a joyous human stream. Every few meters some of them peeled away, spread out blankets alongside the path, plopped themselves down, took lids off containers of food, ate quickly with their chopsticks, sang karaoke songs off-key. Coats were being shed, belts loosened, people were taking off shoes. I felt suddenly lonely, completely alone, filled with loneliness to the depths of my being. I had to leave Japan, but where would I go and would my husband leave, too? The smog had dissipated and the sky, a deepening blue, was touched at the horizon with rose. All of Tokyo had come to picnic in Ueno Park and even now were dropping crumbs everywhere, throwing away food for the crows to eat. The crows could have a feast. The crows could live on the leavings of these picnics for weeks. But there were none to be seen, and my students had disappeared too.

I walked past the giant bronze statue of General Taigo walking his bronze dog on a bronze leash. The lacquered red sides of Kiyomizu temple gleamed. My panic grew. At home my husband would be laying out my dinner, each item lovingly prepared and then placed in its separate dish. He would be worried if I didn't come home. I stepped off the path and leaned against a tree. There was a shoe, a black shoe such as a salaryman might wear, perched at the height of my head on the trunk where it branched. Two shoes, attached to two ankles, clad in white socks. On the side of the socks Snoopy as the Red Baron flew, scarf and long ears streaming behind him, doghouse flying through the air. My heart thumped. It was Mr. Hara. It had to be Mr. Hara. What was he doing up in a tree? I didn't know. It didn't matter. As long as he kept wearing his Snoopy socks he would survive the grind of Tokyo life. The long hours at work. The eleven months and two weeks of the year in which no cherry blossoms bloomed. His tiny Chiba house, his long commute, the loss of his rope. I reached up to touch his foot. But then I let my hand fall away. It was time to leave, to disappear into the crowd, to go without being seen. I turned and started walking away.

"Mrs. Rosenboo? Mrs. Rosenboo?"

I slipped behind the massive trunk of an old cherry tree. Mr. Hara kept calling my name. I peeked out and saw Miss Tanaka's glowing face. She held her dictionary to her breast. She had obviously not seen me, because she was smiling into Mr. Kikuchi's eyes and he was smiling into hers. Mr. Hara swung down from the tree, but Miss Tanaka and Mr. Kikuchi didn't look his way until he began to speak.

"Did you find her? I can't see her from this tree. The sun is almost down. It's difficult to see."

"We asked everyone!" Miss Tanaka said, loud and clear. "We asked, did you see a tall foreigner? From the front she looks like an English teacher, but from behind she looks like a Japanese."

"Sayōnára," I whispered. "Sayōnára." Velvet blooms, small and fragrant, brushed against my hair. I tore my gaze away from Miss Tanaka's happy face and looked up and up and up, as high as my sight would reach. In the unabashed mass of flowers, the pink and velvet abundance of hundreds of cherry blossoms in bloom, I saw the jaunty black feathers and sharp eyes of the crows, dozens of them, some huddled together, some walking along the branches with their tails trailing behind them like princely robes. I cried out and they took wing. They ascended cawing into a sky glimmering black and crimson and gold. Petals fell like pink rain. I watched the crows fly until they blended with the black of the night and there were only stars to be seen, and for a moment I felt comforted because I knew that Mr. Kikuchi and Miss Tanaka and Mr. Hara were watching them too.

In memory of Zita Ohe

Pair Palace

Mrs. Koyama's kettle failed to whistle, as it had every morning for the seven weeks I'd been staying in the six mat tatami apartment of a German friend of mine who was snorkeling in Hawaii with her Japanese boyfriend, but who up until her recent graduation had been a sober student of Meiji era history at the University of Tokyo. My own husband was in India teaching shiatsu at the Indo-Japanese Association of Pune. We had been fighting so much before he left that he didn't invite me along, so when Ingrid offered me her central Tokyo apartment for the winter to "have a change of environment and escape from that rural Saitama hell you live in," I had packed my mountaineering backpack and taken over Ingrid's room. I knew that her apartment had a squat toilet and that I'd have to use the public bath two streets over since the apartment had no bath of its own, but not that her downstairs neighbor's kettle screamed at 5:00 a.m. or that, fifty-eight minutes later, the neighbor turned her radio up to seventy decibels (she was hard of hearing) to listen to NHK's radio exercise program. After a while, I'd hear thumps as she did her jumping jacks. She was ninety-two years old.

But this morning, all was quiet below me. I poked my nose out of the quilt, to test the cold air, to listen for Mrs. Koyama's rapid steps below me. Mr. Ono, who lived in the apartment next door and was, at eighty-five, a babe to Mrs. Koyama, pulled aside his window shutters with more vigor than was needed. They slammed into place, a loud reminder to Mrs. Koyama to set her kettle on the stove, an alarm clock that always came after the alarm clock she had provided me since creation. What if she had died in her bed?

"Something's wrong with Mrs. Koyama," I said to Ingrid's cat Brownie, whom I talked to all the time since nobody else was there. "I don't hear a peep out of her, do you?" I threw off the quilt and Brownie hissed and swished her crooked tail and bounded to the other side of the room. I stood, stunned by the frigid air trickling in through the building's wooden walls, then shoved my feet into Ingrid's Hello Kitty slippers, pulled her fluffy yellow robe around me, and raced down the apartment stairs, where I shivered in front of Mrs. Koyama's door, willing myself to knock, steeling myself for Mrs. Koyama's suspicious voice calling out, "Who's there?"

I knocked. I knocked, although Mrs. Koyama had, for the seven weeks I'd been living above her, expressed unhappiness at my presence, that of a large American woman with a heavy tread. Soon after I'd moved into Ingrid's room, I'd overheard her saying to Mr. Ono that I was wearing my shoes in the apartment, and Mr. Ono, true to his name, had exclaimed the Japanese equivalent of "Oh no!" I had then tried to appease Mrs. Koyama, speaking to her in the best Japanese I could muster, even attempting to use keigo, respect language, which required enough concentration to remember which tongue tripping syllables had to be added onto the ends of common words. I bowed to her when I passed her in the hall, or when I came up the apartment stairs, or if I saw her on her little bronze bicycle, peddling slowly down the street. I offered to carry grocery bags for her. I remarked on the weather. I called her "Koyama-sama" instead of "Koyama-san." All to no avail. She perfunctorily returned my greetings, if she returned them at all. More often, she looked at me as though I were a wild animal that ought to be caged. On the rare occasions she spoke to me, she either complained that I was incorrectly disposing of my garbage or asked when Ingrid was coming home. I had begun spending far too much time sorting and packaging my trash and recyclables in accordance with the eight page booklet of regulations put out by the Minato-ku ward office. I tiptoed around Ingrid's room, trying to make my large self lighter.

"You shouldn't do that," my friend Linda scolded me during a break in our morning Japanese class, when we were standing by "The Boss," the hot drinks machine. "You shouldn't be quiet for her. She's not quiet for you." Linda pointed out that everyone else in the building was affable, that even Mr. Ono, who had been a Morse code operator in the Japanese Imperial Army where he had been taught to hate foreign devils, was friendly, talking with me for a long time. "As if," Linda pointed out, "you were his granddaughter."

"He's lonely," I said. "That's why he talks to me so much."

"No, it's because you're a nice person." Linda took a small but noisy sip from her can of hot Boss coffee. "Too nice, if you ask me. At her age this old lady should have manners and she should mind them."

I didn't tell Linda about the note Mrs. Koyama had recently slipped under my apartment door, asking me to please speak to myself in a quieter voice. The note had taken me an hour to read using both my hiragana and kanji dictionaries. After reading it, I had been unable to sleep. I had lain in my futon, shivering despite the thick quilt over me and the dubious warmth generated by Brownie, who swiped at me with her claws whenever I rolled over onto her side of the bed, explaining to Mrs. Koyama in my head that I wasn't talking to myself but to a cat and that I never had worn my shoes indoors and never would. During a break in the explanation, I considered whether or not I should move back into the apartment I'd shared with my husband before he'd jetted off to South Asia. That apartment was in a modern concrete building called a "mansion" in Japanese-English, and consisted of two rooms, a tiny kitchenette, and an airplane-sized Western bathroom, which was one room and one mini-kitchen and one Western style toilet more than Ingrid's apartment. However, I had promised to care for Brownie and keep her hidden from the neighbors since no cats were allowed. What's more, I had grown used to the squat toilet and felt it was good for my bowels as well as my knees.

"Which?" Linda asked. "The bowels or the knees?"

"Both," I said and added, "How does Mrs. Koyama do it? Most ninety-two year old Americans can barely bend enough to sit down in a chair, let alone squat."

"She has been doing it all her life. I bet she has been rude to foreigners all her life, too."

"I doubt she has had much contact with foreigners except for Ingrid."

"You don't know that. Maybe she has. Maybe she hates Americans, which is strange, since the Japanese like us so much."

"You have to wonder why, since we bombed the hell out of them during the war."

"Don't move back to Saitama because of her. She's an old lady. What can she do to you?"

"Keep complaining. Get me in trouble. Get Ingrid in trouble, too."

"She won't get you in trouble. She'll just continue bugging you about wearing your shoes when you're not and other stupid things. Stand up for yourself. Don't let her push you around. Push back."

I was not a pusher. I could not even push Brownie out of bed when she scratched, or knock loudly on Mrs. Koyama's door. Instead I rapped, a slight rap, more of a tap, with hardly enough force behind it to crack an egg. "Mrs. Koyama?" I called out softly, so as not to disturb the other neighbors since it was only 5:10 a.m. "Mrs. Koyama, are you there?"

Silence and then footsteps on the stairs. Mr. Uchida appeared dressed in a suit and carrying a briefcase. On the bottom step he caught sight of me and froze, his feet in the light dusting of snow that I suddenly noticed was blowing in the open front door and down the hallway to where I stood in front of Mrs. Koyama's door. It was the first time I had really gotten a good look at him, since he left early, came home late, slept in on weekends. Unlike Mr. Ono, who occupied the apartment to my right, Mr. Uchida, who lived in the apartment to my left, very carefully slid aside his shutters and never banged things anytime of the day or night. His kettle never whistled. He was thin, I saw now. Spectrally so. You could practically see through him. My grandmother would want to fatten him up. Anyone would want to fatten him up. He stared at me as if I were the apparition, not he, then lifted his briefcase and clutched it to his chest like a shield. "I don't speak English," he squeaked.

"Something's wrong with Mrs. Koyama," I said, although he was clearly alarmed at the sight of me, who knew why, since he had seen me before. "I always hear her in the morning but this morning I haven't heard anything. I'm worried about her. She could be sick in there."

"No English." His voice sounded as if it had yet to deepen. He had to be my age, but he looked all of fifteen. "No English, only Japanese."

"I'm speaking Japanese. It's Mrs. Koyama. She isn't answering her door."

"The old lady?"

I nodded, shifting from one Hello Kitty slipper to another in a vain attempt to stay warm.

"She must be sleeping," Mr. Uchida said without lowering his shield. He peered anxiously over it at me. Maybe it was the robe. I probably looked like a large yellow chick, Big Bird on the loose.

"She never sleeps this late," I said. "Old people don't sleep late. My eighty-two year old grandmother vacuums at three in the morning. Used to. We took her vacuum away." I was babbling. I couldn't stop. You tell people too much, my husband always complained, but he wasn't here to monitor what I said. "Old people have habits. Routines. They do things the same way day after day. She might be sick in there. She might be dying."

"She probably went away." He stepped gingerly onto the landing as if expecting it to collapse under his weight. "She took a trip."

"In the middle of winter? Where would she go?"

"Someplace warm. I got a phone call this morning. Did you get a phone call this morning?" He was shivering. I could almost hear his bones rattling. My own teeth were chattering. We were a bunch of wussies. Cold wussies. We could wake up the dead with all our noise. "It was the ya—"

"I'm worried about Mrs. Koyama," I interrupted, then added "get out of my way" though he wasn't in my way in the least. I tightened the belt of Ingrid's robe, made a fist, and slugged Mrs. Koyama's door. Mr. Uchida jumped back. Someone needed to feed him. He was Kafka's hunger artist. Skin and bones. I banged again. The door next to Mrs. Koyama's opened instead and Miss Matsumoto poked her head out of her apartment. She was a student at Sophia University, always perfectly made up and accessorized, with belts matching shoes and shoes matching outfits and purse matching it all. At night she often stood outside the apartment house smoking and paging through fashion magazines. Young men sometimes trailed her, heads down, like faithful dogs following their master. These young men were always quiet and she was always chattering. She looked at us bleary eyed, her face bare of makeup, her long hair pinned haphazardly on her head. "What's going on?" she asked in a groggy voice.

"Do you speak English?" Mr. Uchida said. "I hope you speak English, because I cannot help this foreigner. I cannot! I have to catch my train." He backed away from me, bowing, leaving snowy footprints on the floor, then turned and ran out the front door.

"What an odd man," Miss Matsumoto said. She frowned in his direction. "It's snowing and he didn't close the front door."

"Something's wrong with Mrs. Koyama. I always hear her making tea in the morning but this morning I haven't heard anything."

"She's noisy, isn't she? But today, no noise. Close the front door." Her own door gave a loud creak as she started to pull it closed.

"Miss Matsumoto! Wait!"

"My name is Yuko," Miss Matsumoto said in emphatic English. "I studied English in Indiana, America. Tear Hot, Indiana. Three years ago, in 1985. Home stay. Host family. They called me Yuko. One nasty boy down the street called me Yuckie but my friends beat him with snowballs. You can call me Yuko, too."

"Tear where?"

"Ter-ror Hot. But it was only hot in July and August. Soon it was cold. Please close the front door." She slammed her own shut.

I did not think she would come back. I faced the blank expanse of Mrs. Koyama's door alone, put my ear against it, listened for a heartbeat. Silence. Nobody was even in there breathing. Perhaps her feet, like mine, had gone numb within snow-sogged slippers and she had been unable to totter to her kettle and set it on the stove. Perhaps with no friend human or feline to keep her warm, she had frozen in her bed. But Mr. Ono was her friend. Every afternoon at exactly 4:45 p.m. he and Mrs. Koyama emerged from the apartment house and clip-clopped on geta-clad feet to the last remaining public bath in the neighborhood and probably all of Aoyama. It was surrounded by spanking new modern buildings, by haute couture stores, by glass and concrete and steel. Its chimney had once towered over the neighborhood, a landmark which still spouted, like a geyser, gusts of smoke and steam. Upon arrival they separated, Mrs. Koyama to the women's bath and Mr. Ono to the men's, though they sometimes called to each other over the high wall which divided the sexes and upon which a perfectly proportioned Mt. Fuji was painted in spring colors of blue and green. I knew this because I had followed them through the streets and past the Pair Palace, twin buildings which stood cheek to cheek and into which many couples disappeared. Mr. Ono and Mrs. Koyama *were* the Pair Palace. The odd couple. The sweet and sour, the hot and cold, differing in their treatment of me. I should run upstairs and get Mr. Ono to come down and knock on Mrs. Koyama's door but my feet were so stiff and cold I could hardly move and there was no more time to waste. I took a deep breath, expanding my diaphragm as I had practiced while studying voice at the Cleveland Institute of Music in my youth and had not practiced since, and bellowed, "Mrs. Koyama. Mrs. Kooo-yaa-ma. Are you there?"

At the sound Yuko sprang from her apartment, fully dressed in black jeans and black leather boots and a long black woolen coat, her long hair brushed to a sheen. "Shh!" she said. "She will be scared!" She swept up beside me, smelling fruitily of perfume, took off one black leather glove, and rapped smartly on the door while calling out in a pleasantly modulated, very polite voice, "Koyama-san, good morning. It's your neighbor, Matsumoto. Are you home?"

We heard the click of a lock and the door slowly opened. A nose emerged and then an eye, Mrs. Koyama's eye, naked without the glasses she usually wore, surrounded by deep wrinkles. The eye blinked several times and Mrs. Koyama said, in a trembling voice, "I won't move. They can't make me. I've lived here since after the war."

"What are you talking about?" Yuko asked, but Mrs. Koyama closed her door. I looked at Yuko, but she only looked past me with a distracted expression on her face and snapped, "Did you close the front door? You didn't close it! I told you to close it!" She charged past me, dropping her glove on the floor, then slammed shut the door. "Why don't we have a lock for this door? In America there are locks for all doors! Even in Ter-ror Hot there were locks for all doors!"

"Yuko?" I said. "What's wrong?" I paused and tried to steady my quavering voice but before I could say another word Yuko growled, "Don't speak to me in Japanese! Just English! I told you English! Not Japanese!" I stared at her, frozen and baffled and hurt. What was wrong with my neighbors? First, Mr. Uchida had told me I was speaking English when in fact I was speaking Japanese, and now Yuko was telling me I shouldn't speak Japanese. Maybe it was something in the hall, something in the air, something in the snow and cold. Maybe it had something to do with me. "You think everything has to do with you," my husband would say if he was here, but he wasn't here. He was in India, where it was warm.

I swallowed. My throat felt sore. I was catching cold. Yuko could be, too. Her eyes were glittery and scared, and the knuckles of her hand, still on the doorknob, had gone white. We could all be coming down with the flu, or pneumonia, or some kind of plague. I needed warm socks. Heat. Hot tea. A trip to Hawaii. I picked up Yuko's glove and edged towards the stairs. I wanted to speak to Brownie. I found it comforting to speak to Brownie, even though she acted as though she didn't understand a word I said. Ingrid probably spoke to her in German. The closest language I knew any words in was Yiddish. My grandmother had often called me a *gitta madel*, a good girl. I put my hand on the railing and my foot on the first stair.

"Where are you going? I have to talk with you!" Yuko exclaimed. I felt a sudden, warming surge of anger that propelled me up the stairs. Ingrid's phone was ringing shrilly, insistently, but when I picked it up and shouted hello into it in English, nobody was there.

"No wonder you didn't get your homework done," Linda said to me later that day, when she was scarfing down a bowl of udon at the noodle shop around the corner from our Japanese school. On either side of us, black-suited salarymen slurped up noodles or puffed on cigarettes or stomped snow off their shoes. "What's up with your neighbors?"

"I don't know, but Mrs. Koyama looked terrified, poor thing."

"Poor thing, ha!" Linda snorted, shaking red pepper flakes into her bowl. "She's been tormenting you for weeks. Maybe she's been tormenting other neighbors, too. Maybe they've complained to the realtor and told her to shape up or move."

"But she's the boss of the building. Of the whole neighborhood. She's lived there forever. And why was Yuko so freaked out too?"

"Who knows. As for Mrs. Koyama, someone must have turned the tables on her, but why should you care? She's made your life miserable. Eat your ramen. It's getting cold." She fished a slice of sweet pork out with her chopsticks and popped it in. We often grabbed lunch before I left for work and she went home to rescue her children from their grandmother's relentless stream of inane baby talk, of which Linda did not approve. She spoke to her children in complete, Texas-tinged sentences. "Ya'll better behave," she told her boys, and they mostly did.

"I'll ask Mr. Ono what's going on tonight. He'll know."

"You spend too much time talking to old people." Linda had gotten blunt with me since giving birth to her second son. "You need to talk to young people."

"I do talk to young people. I talk to you."

"I don't count. I have children. You should be having them too, but it isn't going to happen when you're sleeping with a cat. When is Sachio coming home?"

"He hasn't said." I stirred my noodles around with my chopsticks before licking the tips. Bad manners. Sachio wasn't around to monitor them. Chopsticks in Japan were exactly the size and shape of the baton I had seen George Szell use to conduct the Cleveland Orchestra with. Maybe he'd licked the tip, too.

"Stop playing with your food. Go home and pen Sachio a missive. Tell him you've made friends in Ingrid's neighborhood. New young friends. Don't mention Ono. Or mention him but knock sixty years off his age. Too bad Oh Yes isn't a name in Japanese. Oh Yes would be better than Oh No. Write Sachio about Ono, but change his name to something else and knock sixty years off his age. And tell him about your other new friends, like what's your neighbor's name?"

"Yuko and she wasn't that friendly."

"I meant the skinny guy on the stairs. Is he cute?"

"He squeaks when he talks. And I'm a married woman."

"So where's the husband? Halfway around the world. Stimulating the acupressure points of God knows who. I have to go." She put her noodle bowl to her lips and drank her soup, then grabbed her purse, plunked some coins on the counter, and disappeared into the swirling snow. Not one drop of broth was left in her bowl. My own was still brimming, my stomach empty, my appetite, despite this, null and void. I drew a pen out of my backpack and grabbed one of the two napkins the counter lady had somehow managed to find for Linda, to pluck out of thin air. The other customers used tissues or their handkerchiefs to wipe their mouths, but Linda insisted on napkins. She sometimes even brought her own.

"Dear Sachio," I began writing on the cleaner of the two napkins. "I'm lonely and miserable and want to know when you're coming home, or if you're coming home, or if you even know." I had nearly reached the end of the napkin which Linda had demanded, but then neglected, to use. She was a fast but neat eater. I was slow and dribbled. I was the one who needed a napkin, needed both napkins, needed a pile of napkins, an armada of napkins, upon which to fit everything I had to say. I pulled my Japanese writing exercise book out my backpack and opened it to a fresh page, staring at the little squares into which you placed one kanji each. They promoted regularity in Japanese penmanship but were not conducive to English script. I switched back to the napkin. At least it was a good-sized napkin upon which I could compose a letter that was longer than Sachio deserved, considering he'd only sent me one postcard to Ingrid's three. Nor had he called, though it was difficult to call from India, requiring a wait of two to three hours at the telephone exchange in a long and sometimes unruly line of men, who smoked or held hands or squatted on their heels, spitting out red streams of betel nut juice. I had done the wait myself, enduring the stares of some young men, the amorous proposals of others, the hot sun, the necessity of peeing with no place to pee, only to reach the front of the line and have the operator fail to establish a connection to America which would have enabled me to break the news to my grandmother that I was going to marry a Japanese I'd met in the Himalayas instead of a Jew I'd met at synagogue, not that I ever went to synagogue. "That's the problem," Grandma told me when I returned to Cleveland and told her about Sachio in person. "You never went to synagogue." She immediately offered to buy me a brand new car in exchange for ditching Sachio. I ought to write him that I'd selected him over a Cadillac.

"Maybe you're never coming home," I wrote instead. "Maybe you're going to wander India forever like a . . ." There was only a tiny corner of the napkin left, large enough to dab a speck of broth from one's mouth if one had eaten any broth, which I had not. ". . . a sadhu." We had seen sadhus, holy men who abandoned hearth and home and traversed India wearing red loincloths and carrying begging bowls, when traveling together after meeting in Nepal on a mountaintop where he had warmed my freezing toes, without once exclaiming over the size of my feet, which had been called platypus feet by unkind children at my elementary school and Jolly Green giant feet by other unkind children, and were always in somebody's way. I had lamented my size since arriving in Tokyo, but now I had better things to think about, such as what was I going to do if Sachio didn't come back from India? Stay in Japan?

I turned the napkin over. There was no time, or space, to turn Mr. Ono into an Oh Yes or to write of the fifteen young people in my Japanese class I talked to every day, sixteen if I included myself, which reminded me that I had yet to think about what I was going to cover in the English class I taught at the NHK Culture Center for a class of well-groomed housewives who always had their homework prepared. I signed "Deborah" in tiny letters, omitting any mention of love, then folded the napkin, put it in my backpack, and placed my sloshy footprints over Linda's crisp imprints as I walked out the noodle shop door. Lunch break over, salarymen and office ladies trudged back to work, heads bowed against the blowing snow. There were no old people out and about. They were probably afraid of the snow. In Cleveland, old people suffered heart attacks while shoveling snow. They slipped on ice and cracked bones. Although born during a Cleveland blizzard, baptized by Lake Erie's wintry winds, I was no longer used to snow and cold.

The snow was a dense mass instead of individual flakes. It fell thickly. Fire engine red taxis crept along Chuo dori, their headlights dim through the curtain of snow. A foolhardy soul wobbled slowly by me on a bicycle, ringing her bicycle bell, short sharp rings like a phone.

"I got a phone call this morning," Mr. Uchida had said. His voice had trembled as he spoke. "Did you get one too?" Who had called him, and who did he think had called me? It couldn't have been Yuko. She had been downstairs, holding the front door closed. She might be standing there still, tightly holding the door with her ungloved hand, preventing someone from coming in. But who?

Inside the Yamanote Line train it was steamy and warm. I felt better until I looked down at the textbook I soon had to teach from, at the precisely rendered illustration of the two Japanese businessmen featured in it, the Misters Sato and Tanaka, cameras in hand, smiling and waving from the top deck of a double-decker bus. They were in London doing something with finance, and had left their wives and children at home.

When not at the office counting pounds and pence they went to see Buckingham Palace, or the Changing of the Guard, or London Bridge. They drank in pubs with their English counterparts and tried English food like Shepherd's pie (which Mr. Tanaka did not like), and fish and chips (which both Japanese men liked). They had conversations about the English weather, the cold and rain. In one lesson their British colleagues took them to a golf course in Scotland, where they shot balls and attempted to understand Scottish brogues. The only women in the textbook were waitresses, a secretary who answered the phone at their office, and a British businessman's wife, who appeared in one lesson to cook the Japanese men Welsh rarebit on toast. What relevance did this have to my students?

Alongside the double decker bus, the River Thames flowed. The sky above was clear. No famous London fog. The sun brassily shone. The men were warm. They had money in their pockets. Bellies full of Welsh rarebit and ale. A year before coming to London they had gone on a sex tour to Bangkok, where they had purchased girls of fourteen, spent an hour or two or three with them in rooms at the same hotel where my husband and I stayed on our way back from India, reservations made sight unseen. The Thai girls wore heavy mascara around deadened eyes and thick lipstick, inexpertly applied. At fourteen I'd been taking voice lessons at the Cleveland Institute of Music and square dancing with a square dance group at old age homes. I saw the Thai girls in the halls and felt ashamed. "Why do you feel ashamed?" My husband asked me, and then said, "It's a release." What's a release? What are you talking about? "It's a release for Japanese men. They work all the time. Sometimes they drop dead from overwork in middle age." Karoshi, it was called. The newspapers carried articles about men who had worked forty-five days straight on a company project, with not a single day off. Died on their forty-sixth day. Soldiers felled in Japan's economic war. Lifetime employment turned death sentence. I couldn't bear to look in the eyes of the Japanese men at our Bangkok hotel. Couldn't bear to look in anyone's eyes, not even my own in the cracked mirror in our hotel room bathroom. I hardly let my husband touch me the four days we were in Bangkok. At night I lay next to him with my fingers in my ears like a child, trying to block out the sounds from the next room.

My head pounded. My throat felt even sorer. The woman sitting next to me leaned over as she fell into a deeper sleep. Her head dropped to my shoulder. I let it stay there. A soft, human weight. What did she do for a release? Shop. Buy designer goods and clothes. Eat expensive food in restaurants. Plan trips to Australia or Guam. I took the train out to the Chichibu mountains on Sunday mornings, while Sachio was still sleeping. From Chichibu station I'd catch a bus and get off at Hanno, hike through the village there, with its old, bent-backed residents, wooden houses with thatched roofs, futons of all colors hung over railings to dry. Women swept the hard earth floor of the old Shinto temple, where a sacred tree grew, an ancient presence, its girth encircled by a braided rope. After the phone had stopped ringing in Ingrid's room that morning, I hadn't been able to get warm. I'd crawled back into the futon, pulled the quilt over my head. In my half sleep Brownie cuffed me with her paw, drawing blood. I awoke with a start. Sat bolt upright until the train arrived at my stop.

"It's like Hokkaido out there," the secretary at the NHK Culture Center said when I arrived in Shibuya. "The radio says it's the snowstorm of the century. We canceled classes. We're telling everyone, don't come, and if you've come, go home. Please be careful and travel back safely."

I turned around. I retraced my steps. Fatigue seeped into my body, my bones. In the lit yellow show windows of the Hanae Mori building back in Ingrid's neighborhood, mannequins with fists on hips smiled waxy smiles. They had long hair. They looked like Yuko. What had she been frightened of? I wondered if the bicyclist I had seen earlier had made it to wherever she was going. The phone had rung sharply like a bicycle bell in Ingrid's room. It might have been my husband calling me. The connection had been bad. We hadn't been able to hear each other. It might have been my husband calling me from India on the telephone exchange phone.

I felt pain like a wound. I wanted to hear his voice. I ran slipping and sliding to Shin-Aoyama station and stood breathless in a line of patient Japanese, waiting for my turn at the yellow-green pay phones that had always looked like play phones to me. When I reached the front of the line I dialed my home phone number in Saitama. The recording my husband made began to play, spoke to me in his voice. The message was rote, familiar, pre-recorded, impersonal. "Kotchira wa Sasaki to Rosenboom-mu desu. Ima gaishutsu shite orimasu no de—" The message was cut off abruptly. A voice, a real voice sounding much like the recorded voice but gruffer, said "Hello." In Japanese.

I pressed the receiver to my ear until it hurt. Two young girls stood behind me, on either side of their mother. They wore matching red wool coats and red hats with dangling tassels. Red boots. There was a puddle at their feet. Snow melting. Or it was me. It was me. It was me melting into the floor.

"Hello?" the voice said again in my ear.

I was hallucinating the snow, the cold, the day, my life, this voice. It had been such a warm voice, but now it was a cool one. It was all because I had lied. My grandmother had offered me a Ford, not a Cadillac. A Ford.

"Who's there? Hello?" the voice on the telephone said. That blue voice. That cool, blue voice.

"Sachio." My own voice was raspy. It came out with no force. I don't know if it came out at all. My throat felt inflamed. I swallowed with difficulty. Tear Hot. Ter-ror Hot. The woman standing behind me looked concerned. She let go of her daughters' hands and reached into her purse. Drew out coins for the phone. She was waiting for me to finish the conversation. She wasn't concerned at all. I had imagined her concern. Imagined Sachio's voice as live. He was in India. Pune, to be exact. Staying at the Christa Prema Seva ashram with the Catholic nuns, with Sister Brigitta from Germany, who had been an Olympic equestrienne and was still strapping and strong, and Sister Sarah from Britain, who had watery eyes that age had leached the color from but a hearty appetite for the perfect round chapattis made by Devika, the Indian cook. She could eat ten of them. Sachio could, too. We had stayed together at the ashram, climbed up on the roof at night to look at the moon. In lust and desperation, we'd locked ourselves into a stall in the men's bathroom. He'd stood on tiptoes to reach my lips. "You're tall," he'd said. "Pretty and tall."

"Who is it? Deborah, is that you?"

I hung up the phone. I replaced the receiver on the hook. Gently, so as not to cause any jarring. I even managed to smile at the mother and her daughters. Then I walked across the station floor. It was wet and gray and slushy, but outside the snow was crystalline, infinite, pure. It burst out of the sky, starry white fireworks, the most beautiful I'd ever seen.

I wandered the streets, lifting one foot out of the deepening snow and then the other. Children in somber navy blue school uniforms threw snowballs at each other, their book bags banging against their legs. I went down the alleyway, past the Sun Merry Bakery and the brand new seven story mansion, where, Ingrid had told me, rich businessmen lived. "They don't hang their futons out to dry in the summer like ordinary people," Ingrid had said. "They probably sleep on beds with canopies around them. That's in fashion. Western beds with ruffled canopies around them. Disgusting." Sachio and I slept side by side on separate futons, in a room so small that in order for me to stretch out my long legs I had to open the closet door to stick my feet and ankles in it. The only time I'd had enough room in bed was when we'd impulsively decided to spend a night in the Pair Palace, which we'd stumbled upon after meeting Ingrid for dinner in Aoyama. We'd rented a room by the hour, with a huge bed smack in the middle of it, surrounded by blue velvet curtains. Blue sheets, blue cover, blue pillows. Blue tinted mirrors on the ceiling. I had looked up when I was lying on my back and seen my stark naked blue-skinned double. A female Krishna, without the flute. I wondered what the interior of the seven story mansion looked like. A businessman's white shirt hung on a top floor balcony, its stiff sleeves outstretched. What was it doing there? Maybe a divorced salaryman lived in the apartment. He had dropped dead of karoshi, but nobody had noticed that he'd left his shirt hanging outside. A frozen ghost, pleading for someone to notice it. A snow scarecrow. A white pelican with outstretched wings.

"You're one wing of a bird, I the other," Sachio had said shortly after we'd met, when he was so romantic he embarrassed me. "Together we fly." He was home and hadn't called me. I'd been too stunned to ask why, or too afraid. He had always been happier in India. It reminded him of a Japan that had vanished but which you could still see in the Tora-san movies, an ongoing series that was wildly popular and which we went to three times a year. We'd watch Tora-san, battered hat on head, smile blooming on his chubby cheeks, leave his family's sweet shop in Shibamata, old Tokyo, on the banks of the Edo river, to wander the countryside helping people in trouble and falling in unrequited love with beautiful women, who responded to him because of his sincerity since he didn't possess wealth or good looks. "That's the Japan of my childhood," Sachio would say, and I'd listen as if I'd never heard him say it before. "People had time. They cared about each other. Now everyone just wants to make money and buy things. They rush here and there." We did too. We both worked six days a week. On Sundays he slept in, while I, desperate for space and green, took the train out to the countryside.

Icicles hung from the eaves of Ingrid's apartment building, sharp, upside-down points, but the steps to the front door had been swept clean and the wooden hallway was as smooth and well-polished as always. Once inside, I tried to pretend that everything was unaltered. Sachio was still in India. Mrs. Koyama was with Mr. Ono at the public bath, like always, scrubbing herself clean before soaking in the tub and gossiping with friends and neighbors.

I went up the stairs. I unlocked Ingrid's door. For the first time ever, I had not folded Ingrid's futon in the morning. I had left it spread out on the floor. Brownie sprawled in the center of it, regarding me suspiciously through slitted gold eyes. "Brownie," I said. "Gitta madel." Her expression didn't soften. After knocking on Mrs. Koyama's door that morning I'd huddled, shaking, before Ingrid's heater. I'd just started to warm up when Yuko knocked on the door. "Can I talk to you?" she asked and I blurted out, childishly, the first thing that came into my head. "Leave me alone." Then listened to her heels on the floor, heavier with each step she took. She needed my help, but I had sent her away. Like Mrs. Koyama, I'd refused to open the door.

I took off my shoes and coat and mittens. I curled up on one corner of the futon. "Have you heard anything out of Mrs. Koyama?" I asked Brownie. My head was stuffed, my voice going. It changed registers within one sentence like a teenage boy's. I'd sleep until next week, next month, next year. At least until Ingrid came home and then I'd decide whether to call Sachio again. If only Yuko would stop talking to me. She kept on talking to me, saying the same thing she'd said this morning: "Can I talk to you, please?"

I jerked awake to knocking at my door. Firm. Authoritative. It increased in volume and persistence. I opened the door to Yuko, still in black like this morning, a Japanese Emma Peel. Her eyes were bright, cheeks rosy, makeup perfect. "I'm very sorry about this morning," she said. "I was rude. I want to apologize and explain everything and cook you dinner."

"You don't have to cook me dinner."

"Oyakodon. Parent-child dish. It's my specialty."

"I have a cold. I better not come over. How is Mrs. Koyama? Have you seen her since this morning?"

"She attacked a yakuza. She's very brave. Shinjirarenai! Look at that kitty!" Yuko kicked off her boots, sprang past me and scooped up Brownie. "You're a sumo kitty catty!" She staggered over with her to Ingrid's kotatsu, sat down, and reached under the kotatsu to plug it in. She lifted the quilt and stuck her legs under it. Brownie flicked her tail once, twice, then rested her large head on Yuko's knee. The room filled with a low, unfamiliar, bass rumbling which took me many minutes to identify as the sound of purring. I stared at Brownie in astonishment. Was this the same animal?

"What's her name?" Yuko asked.

"Traitor."

"Pardon?"

"Brownie."

"Brownie. Brownie-chan. You're much bigger than Koyama-san's neko. You could beat her up. But Koyama-san wouldn't let you. She loves her Mi-chan."

"Mrs. Koyama has a cat?" I said. A jet black cat with burrs in its fur and a bald thrashing tail appeared in my mind. Mrs. Koyama's cat. A witch's familiar. With its back hunched, it faced me, hissing.

"Yes and Ono-san told me she beat a yakuza for it. This afternoon. He said she feels less afraid but he feels more afraid because the yakuza must be angry at her. They will feel ashamed they got beat by an old lady and maybe they will retaliate. She's so brave. Do you have anything to eat?"

"Did you say a yakuza? A Japanese yakuza?"

"What other kind of yakuza is there? They're doing jiage against us."

I sat down. I stuck my legs under Ingrid's kotatsu and planted my elbows on it. The image of Mrs. Koyama's cat, ready to pounce on me, was replaced by the crew cut, thick arms and swagger of the man in my

Saitama neighborhood who often accompanied young Filipina women down the street. Sachio called him a chinpira. A "cheap yakuza." The lowest on the yakuza totem pole. "What's jiage?"

"Ji means real estate." Yuko traced a Chinese character in her palm with her forefinger. "Age is"

"Ageru? To take? To pick up?"

"That's right. The price of land in Tokyo is sky-high. The owner wants to sell the land under the apartment building and get rich, but he has to get rid of us first so he can tear down the building. That's why he hired the yakuza. They'll offer us a bribe to leave but if we refuse they will do bad things to scare us away. It's called jiage."

"Why does the owner have to sick the yakuza on us? Why doesn't he just evict us all? Tell us to move?"

"The law in Japan is very strict. You cannot expel renters easily. The yakuza called Mrs. Koyama this morning. They called me, too, but I thought it was one of my boyfriends teasing me and hung up. But when Mrs. Koyama answered her door this morning, I realized the yakuza had called her and me too. That's why I wanted you to speak English. If the yakuza were nearby, they wouldn't understand. Now do you get it? I'm hungry. I'm not used to all this explaining. Do you have a hamburger or something?" With a grunt Yuko lifted Brownie off her lap and went over to Ingrid's tiny refrigerator. She peered inside. "This is terrible! What do you eat?"

"Why didn't you tell me all that this morning?"

"I couldn't think. I was scared. Can I eat these pickles?"

"They've been in there since Ingrid left for Hawaii. Mr. Uchida was talking to me about some phone call he got this morning."

"It must have been the yakuza calling him. They'll call you too. Brownie's starving! Poor kitty!" I got up and dumped cat food into Brownie's bowl. She ate it ravenously.

"The yakuza came over this afternoon when I was at my university. Ono-san told me they knocked on Koyama-san's door. It's unusual, because their first strategy is to call. But I guess they called Koyama-san and offered her money if she would move out but she refused and yelled at them. Later she got scared, and that's why she acted strangely this morning." Yuko lifted the lid of the rice cooker. "Can I have some rice? Do you have seaweed?"

I pointed to the one shelf that served as a kitchen cupboard. "So the yakuza were here this afternoon?"

Yuko grabbed a rice bowl and pair of chopsticks. "One yakuza. When he knocked on Mrs. Koyama's door she thought it was me or somebody else. Maybe you. The big foreigner. She opened her door and her cat ran out and the yakuza kicked it. Koyama-san got rage and bad temper and hit him with her teapot."

I clamped my hand over my mouth to hold back a snort of laughter. Mrs. Koyama had beaned a yakuza. She had beaned a damn yakuza. She had guts. He might have a ferocious headache. He might have taken to his futon. He might be laying there now dizzy, unable to move.

"The yakuza ran away, but so did Mi-chan." Yuko heaped her bowl with rice, shook seaweed and sesame seeds on it, and carried it over to the kotatsu. "Straight out the front door. Mrs. Koyama spent all afternoon looking for her in the snow. She's in her futon now and won't get up. Ono-san is worried about her. He wants to take her to a doctor but she said she must wait for Mi-chan."

"It's snowing like crazy. How far could the cat have gotten?"

"Mi-chan is like owner. She's in good condition for her age with stamina. She must be hiding or looking for a fish shop. Will you help me look for her tomorrow morning? We should look now, but I'm too hungry."

"Of course I'll help you, but what are we going to do about the yakuza?"

"Koyama-san set us a good example," Yuko said with her mouth full of rice. "Maybe we should fight them with her as our leader."

"I think we should call the police."

"They won't do anything. The real estate owner has too much power. The yakuza too." She put a clump of rice in her palm and held it out to Brownie, who ate it enthusiastically. "She's still hungry. Me too! There's not enough to eat in here for a big girl like you. Is that my glove?" She sprang to her feet, snatched her black leather glove off the bathroom doorknob, and pulled it on. "Yes it's mine!" She bent over, kissed

Brownie on the top of her head, then pulled on her boots. "Knock on my door tomorrow morning and we'll look for Mi-chan. See you then!" She sailed out the door with a cheery good night. I watched her go down the stairs, ponytail bouncing, heels clicking smartly.

"It's just you and me," I said to Brownie. I rinsed out her bowl and put more cat food in it. I picked up the phone and called Linda.

"Abandon ship!" Linda exclaimed after I'd told her what Yuko had said. "Go back to your perfectly nice apartment in Saitama where you can sit on the toilet seat like a proper American. Listen, the baby's about to scream bloody murder so call me tomorrow." She hung up. There was so much to tell her. I hadn't even started. "What are you fighting about?" she had asked me shortly after Sachio went to India. We don't fight. "Sure. That's why he went to India for three months and left you here." He didn't leave me here, I have a job. "Quit it and go to India. See the Taj Mahal or something." He's not anywhere near the Taj Mahal, he's in Maharashtra. "Wherever the hell that is." Plus I wasn't invited. "You're his wife. You don't have to be invited. You can barge in on him if you want to." You sound like my grandmother. "Don't change the subject. Barge. Barge away. It would be good for you. You're too damn polite. You weren't like this last year, or the year before, or the one before that. Last year you would never have let an old lady bully you." She's even bullying the yakuza now, I should have told Linda. She had whacked one on the head with her tea kettle. She was courageous or a fool, I didn't know which. I was one or the other. Most likely the latter.

I blew my nose. I salted a glass of water and gargled. Brownie walked over to the little mat in front of the door and sharpened her claws on it. I squared my shoulders and dialed my home phone number. "It's Deborah," I said when Sachio answered.

"Did you call me this afternoon?"

"Yes, but I was so shocked you were there I hung up. What happened? When did you get back here?"

"A few days ago."

"Why didn't you call me?"

"Do you have a cold? You sound bad. We can talk later."

"I want to talk now."

"I was going to call you when I was prepared."

"Prepared? What for?"

"To tell you. The Indo-Japanese Association asked me to stay and teach Japanese classes and shiatsu. They said they'd help me get a visa for a year."

"A *year*? You mean you're going to do it?"

Brownie was pacing back and forth, like a lion in a cage. She must want to go outside. She must hate being stuck all day in a six mat tatami room. If I opened the door, she'd run away. She wouldn't come back. I'd never see her.

"What about me?" I said.

"You aren't happy. I don't think you like me anymore. You didn't write me."

"I wrote you today. You didn't write me either. All you did was send that postcard of a water buffalo."

"I thought you liked water buffalo."

"I do, but you could have written me a letter. You could have called me from India. You could have called me whenever it was you got here." I bit my lip to stop the stream of words. Sachio had always accused me of being oshaberi. Talkative. It wasn't a compliment. "You could have called me," I couldn't help repeating. I smoothed the quilt that lay over the kotatsu. It was made of a particularly beautiful fabric, a pale gleaming cream dusted with pink peonies, large and swollen with blooms. The most beautiful thing in an otherwise spare room, a monastic room with a futon and kotatsu and several stacks of thick books on Meiji history. Two small burners upon which to cook something. One shelf holding two plates, and one cup, and two pairs of chopsticks. A photograph of Ingrid's parents standing shoulder to shoulder in front of the Berlin wall and a postcard she had mailed from Hawaii of hula dancers.

"You pretend you're okay when you're not," Sachio said. "You don't tell me anything."

"You're not the most communicative person, either."

"You should know my feeling. You married with me."

"I'm not a mind reader."

"I liked you because you were different. You were direct, not like Japanese women. But now you hide things. You changed."

"What if I had come back to the apartment to get something? I would have found you there and been scared. I would have thought you were a burglar."

"How silly. You would know it's me. And Japan is safe."

"Who says it's safe? We're getting harassed by the yakuza here. They're calling and knocking on our doors. They're threatening old ladies and their cats. I don't feel safe. I don't feel safe at all." I wasn't going to cry. I was going to stop myself from crying. I wasn't even going to start. I closed my hand over one of the pink peonies. If it was real I might crush it. I didn't want to crush it.

"The yakuza? Our yakuza?"

"They're doing jiage against us."

"Wow," Sachio said. He had learned to say wow from me. "They'll bother you until you leave. They'll put garbage in front of your door, or come over and play loud music. You'd better get out of there. Come home. Come home now."

"What home? You won't be there. It's not home anymore and plus I have a cat to take care of. I think we should both leave. Go to America or someplace and start over." As soon as the words were out of my mouth I wanted to take them back. He was leaving. Had left. And not with me. "Were you just going to come here, and leave again, and not tell me?"

"I told you I was going to call when I was prepared."

"If they asked you to stay, what are you doing back here?"

"I'm packing up things I need." I could hear from Sachio's voice that he was crying. In the four years we'd been together, he'd only cried once, when he'd told me how his mother, weeks after her stroke, had briefly come out of her coma and asked him where she was. In the hospital, he replied, but she kept repeating the question until, he didn't know why, desperation or the hope he saw in her eyes beneath the fear, he'd lied and told her she was at home. She hadn't asked again. She'd died soon after.

"Deborah? Are you still there?"

"I have to hang up," I rasped. I ran into the bathroom and threw up four times. Once, it occurred to me as I was leaning against the wall crying, for every year of my marriage. At least, if my stomach was keeping count, we hadn't been married for eight years or ten or twelve or fifteen. At least I wouldn't get so dehydrated from vomiting I'd have to be put on an IV. I had a sudden, comforting thought of being immersed in a hot bath up to my chin. How wonderful it would feel. I'd go to the public bath. I'd soak in the hot water and my stomach would unclench and I'd forget about the yakuza and Sachio and Mrs. Koyama and how mean Brownie was to me, and how nice to Yuko. I wouldn't think about anything. I would become dumb and pure and clean. If only I could go to the public bath without being in public, without being goggled at for my height, my large nose, my body hair, my pale skin. It was after 10:00 p.m. Perhaps nobody would be there, and I'd have the whole bath to myself. I could close my eyes and soak. Clear my large stuffed nose with steam. If only I could stop crying. I had in my backpack a delicate handkerchief, made of the finest cotton, given to me by my NHK Culture Center English students. It could not cope with my crying. It did not possess enough volume, enough substance, to cope with my crying. Mrs. Koyama had been strong. I had to be, too.

I walked around Ingrid's room, staggering as if I were drunk, though I hadn't eaten or drunk a thing. I finally pulled myself together. I threw soap and a towel into the bucket I always carried to the public bath, and stepped out into the hall with it. The cold was a shock. It made my nose tingle. When had I last been warm? An image came to me of a woman lying on her back with her legs spread like a Thanksgiving turkey on a platter and her husband on top of her, thrusting not the slightest bit tenderly into her. A knife into flesh. A fork into meat. A ferocious devouring, leaving not one morsel. Well, one. It was growing now, it was multiplying. When he'd groped for me in the dark the night before he went to India, I'd been so astonished, so needy for affection, so careless, so desperate because it had been two months since we'd had sex that I'd left my diaphragm in its little pink box, washed and dusted prettily with corn powder, and pulled him to me. That's when I'd last been warm.

I dropped the bucket. It hit the hallway floor with a clatter. The bar of soap flew out but I didn't retrieve it. I saw a flicker of movement out of the corner of my eye and jumped but it was only Mr. Uchida, sticking his head out of his door. The fear in his eyes subsided when he saw me. "You dropped your bucket," he said, but I ran back into Ingrid's apartment and shut the door. I squatted in front of the toilet and wretched but nothing came out and when I finally stopped I stood up and inspected my breasts in the mirror. They looked larger than usual. The nipples brown and tender. I should have known, but I always skipped periods when I had a change in routine, and moving into Ingrid's apartment had been that change. Sachio and I had done it wordlessly, in heated silence, as if not to acknowledge who we were, or what we were doing. In the morning, before leaving for the airport, he'd pulled me to him in a brief embrace and then pushed me away and afterwards I'd stood under the shower in our bathroom, the tiny tubular shower, washing myself with the brand of soap he used, with the name that always made me chuckle. Cow Beauty Soap, it was called. It had a picture of a black and white Holstein on the package with full udders. Hot water and semen and Cow soapsuds had run down my legs.

I felt my stomach. It seemed to be the same size as usual. Too large. Sachio had been gone seven weeks which meant I was seven weeks pregnant and I knew I should call him back and tell him but instead I stood over the rice cooker and dipped right into it with my chopsticks. I ate the rice, not even bothering to put it into a bowl. When I had eaten every last grain I unplugged the cooker and lay down on Ingrid's futon. "I think I'm pregnant, Brownie," I said. She cautiously approached me. She sniffed my face and hair. It was the first time she had willingly come near me, but I didn't care. "What am I going to do?"

I fell into a feverish sleep. I dreamt that Mrs. Koyama was a young geisha dressed in a rich silk kimono, her hair elaborately arranged on top of her head and kept in place with ivory combs. She carried a fan, which she kept constantly in motion when not strumming her shamisen to polite applause from an audience of yakuza, who sat three rows deep before her while she performed in a Japanese tea house. They all had white shirtsleeves rolled up over their tattooed arms and missing pinky fingers. I circulated among them, pouring tea. My husband sat in their midst, in seiza, dressed in his formal men's kimono, a silky charcoal gray. I tilted the teapot over his cup and snow poured out. "I can't drink this," he said. "Haven't you learned anything since you've lived here?" He grabbed the teapot from me and threw it at Mrs. Koyama. A cat leapt in front of her and took the hit. Mrs. Koyama shrieked. The teapot screamed, only it wasn't a teapot but a baby, long limbed, its mouth open and pink.

I woke with a start. I was drenched in sweat. It's Mrs. Koyama's tea-kettle screaming, I told myself to quiet my racing heart. The room had gone dark. I switched on a light. Brownie's terrified eyes peeked at me from under the kotatsu. I went down the stairs holding tightly onto the railing. The screaming got louder as I descended and I knew that something terrible had happened even before I saw Yuko screaming in front of Mrs. Koyama's door.

My heart might burst through my chest. I put my hands over my face and when I took them away Yuko had stopped screaming and Mr. Ono was standing in the doorway with her, crying out Mrs. Koyama's name. I looked past him into Mrs. Koyama's apartment, to the kitchen countertop where a fat rice cooker sat, red light blinking on its panel. An old framed black and white photograph of a young man in a military uniform stood on the altar in one corner of the room. Offerings of oranges and rice and Japanese bean sweets were heaped before the photograph, colorful against the glossy dark wood. Mrs. Koyama lay on her back in her futon, eyes closed, tiny under her quilt. Mr. Ono stumbled by Yuko and knelt beside her. A cat was crouched facing us in the open window, a fluffy black and orange and white cat with startled eyes and a magnificent, swishy tail. White flakes swirled in. It was still snowing.

I closed my eyes and when I opened them the cat had disappeared and Yuko was leaning out the window, calling its name. The window was up as far as it could go. Mrs. Koyama must have opened it, leaned out, called her cat as if calling a long-lost love, pleaded for it to come home.

I turned away. I burst out crying. Yuko flew to me, grabbed my arm, and pulled me through the crowd of neighbors that had assembled in the doorway and were spilling into the room. She pulled me past Mr. Abe, a middle-aged, single man who traveled frequently to Thailand and Indonesia, doing something with fish farming, and nearly knocked over Miss Kajikawa, who worked as a hostess in a Shinjuku bar and was crouched on her heels with her arms wrapped around her legs. She dragged me by Mr. Uchida, standing in the hallway, looking thinner than before in too-large brown checked pajamas, his mouth opening and closing like a fish gasping for air, and into her apartment. It smelled of chicken and eggs and soy sauce, a normally sumptuous smell that now made my stomach lurch. Okyakodon. The parent-child dish. I'd almost forgotten I was pregnant. I cried harder. "Stop crying!" Yuko barked. Her own face was smudged and streaked with tears. She looked like she'd climbed down a chimney. She emitted fury and the odor of cigarettes. She snatched up her phone, jabbed at the dial pad, and spoke in such rapid Japanese that her words were a blur.

"Mrs. Koyama's dead," I said. "And I'm pregnant." She put her hand over the receiver several times and tried to shush me but I couldn't stop talking. We kept on talking, the two of us, in our own languages and dueling stories until the din grew unbearable. Finally she put down the phone.

"Mrs. Koyama isn't dead," she said, interrupting whatever I was say-ing. I didn't even know myself.

"But I saw her," I sobbed. "I saw her lying there. I didn't do anything."

"How do you know she's dead? Are you a doctor? I called an ambu-lance. They'll come. They'll tell us her condition."

"I didn't help Mr. Ono, either."

"Other neighbors are there to help him, but I need your help look-ing for Mi-chan." She yanked open drawers and tossed clothing at me. My knees buckled. I sank onto something soft and woolen. I could hear the neighbors in the hallway, the pitter-patter of footsteps, voices calling back and forth.

"You want me to look for a cat?" I said. "Now?"

"She's not used to snowstorms. She's old and scared. She will die out there and then if Koyama-san survives she will die a second time of heartache, I mean break."

"It's dark. How are we going to find her?"

"Tokyo has lights everywhere. We can look for her footprints in the snow and follow those." Yuko tugged at the sweater I was kneeling on. "My homestay mother knitted this but it was always too big for me. Stand up! Put it on! You can't go out in pajamas."

I stood up. "These aren't pajamas, they're my clothes. I fell asleep in them."

"You need more fashionable wear."

"Nothing here fits me."

"You haven't looked hard enough. And you could put on makeup. You could fix your hair." She took off her nightgown and pulled on jeans and a sweater. She drew on her coat and started to button it. "How do you expect to get a boyfriend?"

"I'm married."

"You are?" Yuko paused in her buttoning and stared at me as if it was the most astonishing thing she'd ever heard. "Where's your husband?"

I ran into the bathroom. I shut the door and wretched over the toilet, then leaned over the tiny sink, a marvel Ingrid did not have in her bathroom, and tried to banish the picture of Mrs. Koyama lying on the floor from my mind, which competed with the picture of the cells in my uterus shaping themselves into a miniature Sachio. Contrary to what I had learned in biology class, they were gray and glassy. Like marbles. Like the eyes of the dead. I shuddered and flushed the toilet again. Japanese women always flushed the toilet to hide the sounds of what they were doing in the bathroom. In some of Tokyo's department store restrooms, you could press a button inside the toilet stall to start a soundtrack of a waterfall, or rain falling, or of a babbling brook, though I'd once pushed the button and heard "Matchmaker, Matchmaker" from *Fiddler on the Roof* played tinnily through the loudspeaker I found near the toilet roll dispenser. They needed a different sort of music for women who were throwing up or crying instead of peeing. Hard rock music, played at eighty decibels. Someone bashing the heck out of a drum set. An amped up electric guitar. A singer singing fortissimo. Yuko needed my help looking for Mi-chan. I leaned over the sink and splashed my face with cold water. Seven weeks of cells that could only, individually, be seen under a microscope probably added up to something the size of my little finger. Or of my fingernail. Maybe I wasn't even pregnant. Maybe I was just late and swelling up with blood and fluid.

"Are you okay in there?" Yuko called out.

She had said, "You could wear makeup. You could fix your hair." Two open makeup bags lay on the little wooden shelf above her sink, overflowing with tubes and bottles and ointments and brushes of all shapes and sizes. There were jars, all with their lids off, containing green or blue or silver or gold mascara, a palate of rich, dressy, shining colors, of shimmering powders. There were brushes of all shapes and sizes, stubby makeup pencils, a contraption I had seen women clamp onto their eyelashes to make them curl. There was a teensy tiny razor, used to shave who knows what from where. If the baby was a girl then she might grow up to be a wearer of makeup, unlike me. She'd be fashionable. She'd be slim and not too tall and fashionable and more Japanese than Jewish. She'd blend in better. She'd have straight hair. I sniffed in the fragrances. I dipped my finger in different potions. I dabbed a flowery smelling perfume at my temples. My nausea subsided. "You feel better," I told myself. "Calmer. You can face the world. You can face murder and pregnancy and the yakuza. You can face Sachio. You can face looking for a freaked-out cat during a snowstorm." Suddenly I realized it had gone dead quiet.

"Yuko?" I said.

I put my finger under the hook to unlock the bathroom door but then I froze. What if the yakuza had come? What if the yakuza were in the building, wreaking mayhem? I had a baby to think of, even if I was later going to get rid of it. I listened intently. I waited for something to happen. When I couldn't stand it anymore I grabbed Yuko's nail scissors and stormed forth. The apartment was empty. I could hear shouts from the hallway. Authoritative sounding men's voices. Through the cracked open door I watched a policeman stride by, his boots clomping on the floor, followed by two men carrying Mrs. Koyama on a stretcher and a procession of my neighbors, with Yuko following. I slipped out into the hallway. Everyone was huddled outside by the police car. I recognized Mr. Uchida, standing there engulfed in his robe. The flashing lights from the police car cast red stripes on his head. He turned and made eye contact.

I shrank back. I leaned against the wall. It was cold, but solid. I rested against it, just for a moment. Salarymen dozed, standing. They swayed as the train moved, never toppling over. Somehow they always knew when their stop came. They sprang out of sleep and into brutal wakefulness. You couldn't be old and slow in Tokyo, though of course people were. I'd see the elderly, struggling to carry their bags and keep their footing while people streamed around them, sometimes colliding, and wonder if that would be me in forty years. Unable to keep up the pace. I didn't want to grow old, like Mrs. Koyama, while the city changed rapidly around me. Now she was dead. The yakuza had killed her.

"She's alive."

There was someone talking to me, blurred, indistinct. I blinked and he came into focus. Mr. Uchida. "The old lady is . . ." he began clearly enough but the end of his sentence disintegrated into a mumble. "I wanted to tell you. Also," he hesitated, reddening, "that I found your bucket. Soap, too." He walked away.

"Wait!" I said to his retreating back.

He half turned towards me. He was way too skinny and his nose was running.

"What did you say about Mrs. Koyama?"

"I put the soap in the bucket. I left it in front of your door."

The man was maddening. I wanted to shake him. Irritation revived me, propelled me towards him. "Mrs. Koyama," I said. "I'm asking you about Mrs. Koyama. Our neighbor. Is she . . ." I didn't know how to put it delicately in Japanese. There must be a way to do it. I went over possible sentences in my mind while Mr. Uchida dabbed his nose with a handkerchief, looking embarrassed and uncomfortable.

"Is she dead?"

"No. I don't think so." It suddenly struck me what an odd conversation we were having and, to my horror, I laughed. I immediately clamped my hand over my mouth but it was too late. Mr. Uchida had heard me. The muscles in his face quivered and I apologized. I said that I was sorry for my poor manners and rudeness and added, for good measure, that I shouldn't have left my bucket and soap out in the hallway where anyone could slip on it, but Mr. Uchida emitted a creaky sound, a cry of outrage. I halted mid-apology. He was smiling. I stared at the smile in astonishment. It broadened his thin face. He looked completely different. Kind. Almost handsome, if much too thin.

"It's funny, but not funny," he said and emitted the sound again, a rusty chuckle, smiling at me so broadly and warmly and completely that I smiled, too. We stood there for what seemed like five minutes while the ambulance siren faded in the distance until I realized that I could not be smiling like this at him. I was married, however tenuously, and pregnant. I could not be smiling like this at him.

I could feel the smile dying on my face. Before I turned and fled, before I turned and went up the stairs, I saw the smile dying on his face, too, going out, snuffed out as if by sudden bad news. I wanted to explain why I couldn't keep smiling but he was a stranger and I couldn't explain a thing.

At the top of the stairs it took me a moment to remember which way to turn until I saw the bucket in front of Ingrid's door. I scooped it up and entered the sanctuary of Ingrid's apartment where I let my smile grow stone cold while Brownie sat on the futon grooming herself, her tongue swooping over her fur. When the phone rang, I knew that I'd been waiting for it to ring. It was the yakuza. Or Sachio. If it was the yakuza, I would yell at them. If it was Sachio, I would yell at him. I picked up the phone. I said hello in Japanese. As harshly as I could, though the Japanese word of greeting used for phone calls was a soft word, as light as a snowflake. Nevertheless, I tried to say "moshi moshi" as harshly as I could.

There was a crackling over the line. A voice said, "Deborah?"

I gulped and practically choked on nothing. On air. Cold air. "Mom?"

"Deborah, is that you? The connection's bad. I can hardly hear you."

"It isn't the connection, I have a cold." Ingrid's big bold German clock was facing me, the numbers bright, illuminated. It was two in the morning. What were my parents doing calling me at two in the morning? Someone must have died, but who? My grandmother. She had been claiming death was imminent. She had finally died, as she had threatened to. I could see her lying in her apartment, in the bedroom which she occupied alone, having, two years previously at age eighty, kicked out my eighty-five year-old grandfather. Lying alone, like Mrs. Koyama. Two old ladies on other sides of the world.

"What's the matter?" my mother said. "Why are you crying?"

"Grandma died. She's dead, isn't she?"

"What are you talking about?"

"Why else would you call me at two in the morning? Just tell me. Just tell me when it happened."

My mother gasped. "Moses!" she said to my father. He was obviously sitting across the kitchen table from her. "Moses! It's 2:00 a.m. not 8:00 a.m. Some math whiz you are!"

"You mean Grandma's not dead?" I said as my father rumbled an apology, basso profundo, in the background.

"Of course not! Why haven't you written? Ever since Grandma's learned to read she keeps asking if there's a letter from you. All you sent was that lousy postcard with your German friend's address and phone number on it. At least I know it's the right number."

"I'm sorry, Ma. I haven't had time to write. There's a lot going on here."

"Like what?" my mother said just as I was about to blurt out that I seemed to be pregnant. "Why are you staying in a friend's apartment? Where's Sachio?"

"He's in India," I said before I could think better of it.

"India!"

"I mean he was in India but now—oh forget it. It's a long story."

"Don't tell me. He kicked you out. You're on the street. Moses, she's on the street."

"I'm not on the street, I'm in Ingrid's apartment."

"Doing what?"

"Taking care of her cat," I said and was going to add that I was also puking my guts out when someone knocked on the door.

"Deborah?" Yuko called out. "Deborah, are you in there?"

"You left your home to take care of a cat?" my mother said.

"We have to look for Mi-chan now!" Yuko called out. She rapped, impertinently.

"You don't even like cats," my mother said.

"Deborah? Deborah!"

"When you were little, you were afraid of cats. Even of kittens."

"Ma, can you hold on a minute?" I covered the receiver and shouted out to Yuko, with as much volume as I could muster, that I was on the phone and would be down as soon as I got off.

"Who are you talking to?" my mother said when I uncovered the receiver.

"Nobody."

"You can talk to nobody at two in the morning but not to your mother?"

"It's my neighbor, Yuko. We're having some problems with the yakuza at our apartment building." I'd spilled the beans. To my mother, no less. I groaned. She and my father were voracious readers. World history, military history, international affairs, politics and biographies. Since I'd moved to Japan, they'd made a point to read everything about it. They'd know about the yakuza. They probably knew more about the yakuza than me.

"The yakuza?" My mother pronounced the word so it rhymed with jacuzzi. She was going to be worried sick. I'd made a big mistake. What was the point of worrying her? She couldn't do anything an ocean and a continent away. "What do you mean problems? What kind of neighborhood are you staying in?"

"A pretty ritzy one, actually. That's why the yakuza are trying to evict us."

"Who, you? You mean they're your landlords?"

"No. I don't know who owns this place."

"Debby, honey, are you in some kind of danger?"

"No. Maybe. I don't know. Of course not."

"I haven't gotten one straight answer out of you. I want you to talk to your father."

"I can't right now. It'll take a while to explain and I don't even understand it that well myself. I have to go, Ma. I'll call you again. I promise. In the morning. I mean the morning here, not there. I'll call you and explain everything."

My mother snorted.

"I have to go, Ma," I said again. "I'm sorry," and hung up the phone. I had been hanging up on everyone. It was a childish thing to do. I put on my coat and hat and boots. The last thing I saw when I went out the door were Brownie's eyes staring at me, two huge, golden, frightened moons.

We looked for Mi-chan. We looked for hours while the snow kept falling and finally came back to the apartment building just as a bluish dawn broke and the snow was nearly up to our knees. We stood outside anyway for a while in the white silence as Yuko tried to light a cigarette before throwing down her matches disgustedly and stamping up the stairs with her cigarette still unlit. I hunched against the cold, calling Mi-chan, and when she didn't come I knew. The knowledge settled over me. I felt ill and tired.

The building seemed deserted. I walked through the silent hallways. "I didn't call her name loudly enough," I said to Brownie, who opened her eyes sleepily when I came in. "I don't know her name. I haven't come up with anything. I can't even see her."

Brownie stared at me blankly. I had spoken to her in English. I had promised someone not to speak in English, but who? Not my baby. The poor baby. An accident. Her father wouldn't be around to talk to her. She wouldn't hear his language, as I had heard it when we'd first fallen in love. Aishiteimasu. His own brand of Japanese, which I'd been trying for years to learn. They didn't teach it in the Japanese school I went to. I'd have to quit going. "We should have had you when we still loved each other," I said to the baby. "I'm sorry."

I crawled under the covers. I heaped on extra blankets. I dreamt that I was making a snowman with Linda, rolling a snowball until it got bigger and bigger and so heavy that we had to lean against it and push with all our might, Sisyphus rolling his stone. I wanted to stop pushing. I begged Linda to let me stop pushing but she said, scornfully, that I was a coward and that there was no other way to give birth but to push out the baby. Sweat dripped off me. Keep on pushing, Linda said. Push with all your might. My sweat melted the snowman in a flood of warmth and wetness and I woke with a start to the smell of ammonia and the sight of Brownie crouched next to me, peeing in the futon.

I scrambled out of bed so fast that Brownie yowled and flew across the room. I tore off my clothes and splashed myself in the icy kitchen sink water. I washed myself frantically, even though I had to pee so badly that I barely made it to the bathroom. I squatted naked over the toilet, peeing out a gallon. "Why are you looking at me like that?" I said to Brownie when she came to the bathroom door. "At least I made it to the toilet which is more than I can say for you." I ripped toilet paper off the roll, and wadded it furiously. "Ingrid never told me you were a bed wetter." Brownie lifted one long leg and licked it. "Don't I treat you well? Don't I talk to you?" The room stank. The room smelled vile, but all Brownie did was lick herself. It was my fault for not putting away the futon. For days, contrary to etiquette and propriety, I had not put away the futon. I had let Brownie lounge there in dissolute splendor and now the futon and futon cover were ruined and Brownie was meowing at me, the same meow she used when she wanted me to feed her. I had been doing nothing but feeding her for the last forty-eight hours. Maybe she was pregnant, too. An immaculate conception, unlike mine. Maybe we'd both do nothing but pee and eat until the yakuza turned us out in the street, and where were they? From where I was squatting I could see

Ingrid's clock. It was three in the morning. I had slept over twenty hours. I had missed Japanese class and missed the English class I had to teach but most likely everything had been cancelled because the snow was still falling. Would it never stop? Just as I was about to stand up a cramp hit me, intense but familiar. I cried out. A gush of blood came out, a frightening volume. A tsunami wave. I was having a miscarriage.

I squatted there gasping until the cramps subsided. I squatted while the blood streamed out, one gush for every cramp, in a painful rhythm that went on and on until my thighs quivered from the strain and when it finally seemed to be over, I could hardly stand up. My knees ached. I felt weak and dizzy. I walked stiffly into the room and lay down on the floor. I pulled my jacket over me and watched Brownie sniff at the blood still speckling the sides of the toilet. I'd have to clean it. I'd have to throw out the futon. I'd have to get dressed. I'd have to open the sliding door and let the frigid air in to dispel the stink of cat pee. And of blood. Of a severing. I'd lost the baby. When kangaroos were born, I remembered from a Wild Kingdom special I'd watched as a child, they crawled upwards from the vagina until they reached their mother's pouch. It was a long journey, given their size. They were red, hairless, almost formless, but they single-mindedly crawled until they were able to seize a nipple. To latch on. Hold on for dear life. It had been a girl. I felt her now in my chest, a lumpy presence. "I'm sorry," I said to her. "I'm sorry."

I lay there for a long time, with my cheek against the scratchy tatami. It was old and yellowed with age. It smelled like popcorn. Bits of it stuck up, like grass that hadn't been cut. It tickled my cheek. It felt like straw. I might almost be in a manger. "I'm not sleeping with you again," I told Brownie. "That era's over with." She flopped onto her back and rolled from side to side. I kept talking to her so I wouldn't go crazy. "I'm not petting you either," I said, though I had never petted her to begin with. She got up and scampered from one side of the room to the other. She seemed full of energy. Piss and vinegar though she had pissed out everything and the stench was so strong I finally got up and pulled on the sliding door. It was frozen shut. Ice had traced lacy patterns on it. I was trapped, smothered by snow and ice and the stink of cat urine. It had soaked into the futon. Ruined it. But at least I could find no blood on anything but me.

I stood at the sink and drank glass after glass of water. I put food in Brownie's bowl, moving in slow motion. I changed her litter box. I wiped the blood off my thighs. I felt between my legs. There was blood on my fingers so I put on a pad and flushed the toilet several times, without looking into the bowl. Instead I watched the arc of water come out of the spout. It came out clear. It wasn't scarlet. It curved over the top of the toilet and fell gracefully into the basin that served as a sink. The whole contraption was a marvel of Japanese engineering. The water that came out of the top was clean, I had been told five hundred times. It's not the same water that is running down the toilet. But nobody had ever explained the mechanics of it to me and I wasn't going to wash my hands in it so I washed them one last time in the kitchen sink until they were clean. She was gone. So soon. Every last trace of her. I hadn't called my mother back. She'd be worried, especially because I'd told her about the yakuza. "They'll harass us until we leave," Yuko had said rather cheerfully while we were out looking for Mi-chan. "When it stops snowing they'll come with their trucks, and play loud music through megaphones. It's a good thing it's still snowing, except that we can't find Mi-chan." As the night waned she'd gotten more cranky and discouraged. At one point she'd sniffed close to my ear and snapped, "Are you wearing my perfume?" I hoped that she wasn't awake. I'd have to sneak by her door. I hoped that she wasn't outside, smoking, and if she was, what would I say to her?

I got dressed. I bundled up in everything. He didn't even know about it. I'd had a one night stand, as it were, with my own husband and he didn't even know I'd gotten pregnant. Now he never would. I wouldn't tell him. I would dispose of the evidence. The futon. I suddenly remembered that futons were considered special items and that there were rules on how and where to dispose of special items. I couldn't just throw it away anywhere but I was not about to crack open my kanji dictionary, to try to figure out how many brush strokes made up each unfamiliar character in the garbage disposal pamphlet. I would dispose of the special item in the area for regular items and if anyone caught me, I would pretend not to speak Japanese. I would feign gaijin ignorance. Mrs. Koyama would yell at me if she saw me. She would yell at me, but then I remembered that she couldn't yell. She was in the hospital.

I slung the futon over my shoulder like a body and went out the door with it. It was five in the morning. Nobody was up at five in the morning but Mrs. Koyama doing her jumping jacks, but this morning she wasn't doing her jumping jacks. She was lying inert in a hospital bed. Or awake, and complaining. She might be drinking green tea. Getting a blood transfusion. I might need one myself. That and an examination but if I went to the doctor I'd have to lie buck naked under a gown which wouldn't fit me while the doctor, most likely a male, looked down my vagina. Cleaned out the last of her. He'd tell me I was young. That my husband and I could have other children. The lump felt heavier. I didn't want to go to the doctor. Neither did she. "You're dead," I said to her. "You can't put in your two cents worth. I miscarried you." I couldn't tell anyone about it. It was a secret. "You don't tell me anything," Sachio had said, and now I wouldn't get the chance to. He was probably on his way back to India.

I crept down the stairs like a thief with my booty and out into the pre-dawn grayness and then I stopped, stunned. The snow rose to the top of the steps and beyond. It lay heaped on the rooftops. Mounds of it, vanilla ice cream. A Shiba Inu, her fox face framed in red fur, looked at me with dark eyes and it took me a moment to realize that she was being carried by someone, who plunged through the drifts, hat pulled low over his forehead, puffing breaths of steam, never once glancing at me. The dog turned her head and stared pleadingly at me as her owner carried her off into white oblivion, but there was nothing I could do. Nothing I had done. The wind stung my face. Somewhere, a piece of metal was rattling. What was mother nature doing, and when would the snow stop falling? Perhaps it would not stop falling.

I stumbled down the front steps, sinking up to my thighs in snow at the bottom. I felt disoriented by white everywhere and only got my bearings when I spotted the green public pay telephone down the street, wearing a chef's hat of snow. Beyond it, around the corner, was the garbage area. I headed towards the green pay telephone. Snow crystals soon clogged my mittens. My jeans became soaked. The snow was heavy. A white barrier. Around the corner from the telephone, the garbage containers in their glossy blue and red and yellow paint seemed the only remnants of human presence. Archeological artifacts. Tokyo felt like a ghost town, one with blowing snow instead of tumbleweed. I stood there in the icy emptiness for a while. I brushed off the brightest container, the yellow one that held cans and bottles, and set the futon down on top of it.

The wind picked up. It blew right through me and I wanted to seek out shelter but I couldn't leave the futon. It looked so lonely there. Discarded. Nobody would ever again sleep on it. It would remain ingloriously and illegally on display in the garbage area until the snow obliterated everything. I picked it up and cradled it to me. It smelled noxious, horrible, pungent, but I held it as long as I could stand to and then set it back down on the container. There was a lithe leaping, a sudden movement, and a cat jumped onto the futon, claiming it. Mrs. Koyama's cat. It was unmistakably Mi-chan, whom Yuko and I had looked for in the wee hours of a rare snowstorm, after being awake for nearly twenty-four hours. We had walked around, looking for her footprints, cocooned in the silent dark, the swirling snow. We had searched in a radius, growing increasingly cold and hungry and exhausted. Now she was right in front of me, rapturously sniffing the futon, her extravagant tail peppered with snowflakes and flicking back and forth. She looked stoned. As if inhaling an aphrodisiac, a perfume. Kitty Christian Dior instead of Brownie's pee. I'd had a miscarriage. Because of Brownie, I'd had a miscarriage. We'd never been a happy pair together in the futon. She'd never purred me to sleep and I suddenly hated her. Loathed her. All cats. I thought of the yakuza kicking Mi-chan and I wanted to kick her too.

"Stay there," I said. She froze and stared at me with her sea-green eyes. I knew I should grab her. I should grab her, and hold her, and carry her back to the apartment house but she might scratch me. She might sense that I hated her and scratch me. If only Yuko would come striding down the alley smoking but the snow was too deep to stride in and it was too early for her to be up. She'd know what to do. She'd be a good kitty snatcher. "Good kitty," I said to Mi-chan. I put my arms under the futon, carefully, like a surgeon inserting his hands into a body cavity but she immediately jumped onto the next garbage can. I picked up the futon anyway.

"You can't leave that futon there," a voice growled at me.

Mi-chan vanished. I whirled around, still holding the futon. It was a yakuza. Three of them.

"Gaijin da!" the littlest one exclaimed. Little Bear. "It's a foreigner!"

He had a startled expression on his little square face which changed to a fearful one as Big Bear said something harshly to him, in men's Japanese, slangy, clipped, the syllables blown away by the wind so that I couldn't hear them. But Little Bear heard. He clamped his lips together, as if determined not to say another word. I could feel my own lips tightening. A current shot through me.

"You can't leave that futon there," Big Bear repeated in his gruff voice. "It's the wrong place."

"She doesn't speak Japanese," Middle Bear said. "She speaks English. In-gurishu, yes?" he said to me. "Yes, no?"

I could bolt. I had long legs. I had always been a good runner. If only my legs didn't feel so tired. They had gone numb. They might be wood. They weren't even tingling. And the snow, in any case, was too deep.

"Something smells," Big Bear said. His big head jutted towards me. I leaned away, pressed my back up against the garbage container. The sky poured snow. I was tired of snow.

"Foreigners stink of butter," Middle Bear said.

"This isn't butter," Big Bear said.

Butter was yellow. A pretty color. The color of the sun, the color of India and heat, of daffodils, of tatami aged from green to gold, of a cheerfully painted child's room.

"She doesn't take a bath," Big Bear said. He looked me in the eye. He knew I could understand Japanese. I looked away. "She's a stupid foreigner who doesn't take a bath." Middle Bear nodded. Little Bear nodded, a littler nod, but his heart didn't seem to be in it. He looked wet and cold. Sticks and stones may break my bones. I would have taught her that. Every child learned it. Had to, because the world was cruel and she would have been teased for looking more foreign than Japanese, for being different, like my friend Bret had been teased in the fourth grade. The first black child at my Cleveland Heights elementary school. Perhaps Little Bear had been born a burakumin, an untouchable, and had joined the yakuza because he had been called stupid so many times, too. Bakka. It was a harsh word, a horrible word that I had not learned from Miss Tachiki, my Japanese teacher, who recited sentences for us to repeat every day in her bell-like voice, and who had tiny feet encased in little slivers of shoes with barely visible straps and high heels, fairy shoes adorned with bows and sparkles and other glittery girlish things, none of which looked warm. On the last day I'd seen her, which seemed so very long ago, she had been wearing slightly more substantial though still stylish footwear, sleek black boots which somehow looked dry and pristine despite the snow. Her toes must be impervious to cold. I wished mine were impervious to cold. I wished that instead of coming outside to dump Ingrid's futon, I had fired up her oil heater. I wished that I hadn't had a miscarriage, even though I knew, after fruitlessly looking for Mi-chan all night, that I would get an abortion. I wished that I was inside, in Ingrid's room, thawing out my toes.

My breath came out in a whoosh. I'd been holding it. Big Bear knew that. It was so cold he could see my breath coming out, a white cloud, a smoke ring. He could see me gulping air in. He could see my chest heaving under all of the layers. He could see my bleeding womb. They won't do anything to you, I told myself. It's morning. It's morning, when you're usually in Japanese class, sitting next to Linda, watching Miss Tachiki take her prancing steps across the room. It's morning, when the housewives come out to sweep their front stoops, when their husbands leave for work. Someone will come by soon. They won't do anything. They won't hurt a woman. They won't stab you, like they did that Socialist Party executive when he was making a speech on human rights. You haven't made a speech on human rights. You haven't done anything. You're a coward with big feet. If only someone would walk by. If only the Shiba Inu would return, with her master. I'd shout for help. She would leap out of her master's arms. Run at the yakuza. Growl at Big Bear. He might be scared of dogs, as I was of cats. Even, as my mother had said, of kittens. But the dog was nowhere to be seen. The storm had intensified. I could only see in a radius of about six feet in all directions. The yakuza were in the radius with me.

"She came out here to sleep," Big Bear said. "She has to sleep out here because she lives in that old wooden shack and has to move out. In a week." He knew where I lived. He had seen me. I stuck out. I couldn't be missed. He kept on talking. I only understood some of the words. There was a roar in my ears. It was the wind. It was the wind, moving through me. The cat had vanished on its current. She wouldn't come back. She had been kicked once, maybe by Big Bear. She was a pretty girl, a little wisp of a thing. So light that when Big Bear had growled at me she'd glided over the snow. Skimmed over the top, the surface of it. Flown, on fleet feet. Run, Mi-chan, run. It was damp between my legs. I'd had a stroke in my womb and it had burst. You're like a rat, Big Bear was saying, or something of the sort. Like a rat coming to the garbage pile to feed.

That's when I dropped the futon and slapped him across the face.

His eyes widened. He put a hand to his cheek. Later, I remembered the exact shape of that hand. As if it had been imprinted in my mind, like my own hand was imprinted on his cheek.

We were all suspended, for a moment, in place.

Middle Bear lunged at me. Big Bear followed. Everyone shouted. I shouted the loudest. Screamed "you bastards." Screamed in fury and they were on me, kicking and hitting me and I crouched over, I crouched over and screamed.

Then, instantaneously, I was high above the surface of the earth, looking down at myself, a speck far below. There were three other specks there with me but I looked away from them, off to where Aoyama dori swept its wide white path through the city. The street was empty but for a lone figure who lifted off the earth as I watched. Flew up with no wings. Came closer until I could see streaming hair, a red backpack, legs still pumping though he'd left the earth. My husband's backpack, on the back of my husband. I'd followed it up many a trail. He'd always surged ahead of me. We had hiked the Japan Alps together. We had climbed Yatsugatake and Yarigatake and Mt. Fuji. We'd huddled together in a tent, eating ramen we'd cooked on a camp stove. He'd stuck needles in the leg I'd broken on Mt. Miyanoura, on Yakushima. My husband, who was ascending towards me, though perhaps not towards me, but towards the top of some mountain. For once I was ahead of him on the trail, and I wasn't out of breath in the least. Just as he came close enough for me to see the anguish in his face I was back in my body, on the earth.

Back. Without falling from my perch. Without gliding down. Without slipping down. Without floating down, like a snowflake. It was a jump.

A huge hopscotch back to earth. Someone skipping stones across water and I was the stone only I hadn't felt myself skip. It was that quick. I was just back and it was over. There, to the right of me, were the familiar garbage containers, a glossy red and yellow and blue. There was the futon, frosted with snow, lying at my feet. And the green public pay telephone, surrounded by snow, by high white peaks. I had come down, from the mountain, from wherever I had been. I felt remarkably well. Refreshed. Calm. I could feel my legs. The blood flowed through them. They no longer tingled and I could walk on them and I did. The Three Bears had disappeared. Vanished. I had dreamt them. They hadn't been real. My husband wasn't real, either. He was a memory of himself, running towards me. He had always been so graceful but in my faulty memory he had become gawky, lifting his legs comically high, as if trying to hop above the snow, his backpack shifting from side to side as he moved. He had overloaded it. He always insisted on carrying our tent, our water, our heaviest things. When I'd broken my leg on Mt. Miyanoura, he had even tried to carry me. Perhaps he had broken his own leg. I felt just the tiniest quiver of fear. Perhaps he had broken his own leg and that accounted for the jerky way in which he ran towards me, the awkward discordance of it, and for the look of terror on his face.

I did not want to remember that look. I looked instead at his hair, bobbing on his back as he ran, like a horse's tail. It was thick hair, coarse hair, but I had loved to stroke it. I did not want to remember that, either. I wanted to hold onto the calm feeling, the refreshed feeling I had. He might have hurt his leg. He needed help. It was useless to panic. I'd broken my leg on the top of Mt. Miyanoura. The fog was so thick I hadn't been able to see my feet. I'd stepped off the trail, into the space made by snowmelt. A deep gash in the earth. The sound of my leg breaking was like a rifle shot. He stayed calm. The whole time. I could, too. "Don't run," I called out to him. But the snow had been tramped down around me by many feet, making his last few steps easy. He didn't stop. He ran right up to me. Stumbled over the futon, righted himself. Seized my arm. Asked, "Are you all right?"

I said, "Are you?"

He didn't answer, couldn't answer. He had to catch his breath and when he did he looked at me with that same look on his face. I kept asking him if he was all right and he kept asking me. We traded off asking each other this, like copycats. It was ridiculous and absurd. When we had finally gotten tired of it neither of us had answered the other though he insisted I must be hurt.

That's when I said, "I'm not anymore. It's all over with."

Then I said, "Remember when we had sex the night before you went to India?"

There was a sheen of sweat on his face. He had always been so handsome, but now he was wet and bedraggled. He held my arm tightly. I couldn't stop talking. Oshaberi. "I didn't use my diaphragm that night. I left it by my pillow."

"They were kicking you," he said. "I ran here as fast as I could."

"It's my fault. I don't know why I didn't use it."

"You aren't wearing mittens." He let go of my arm and took both my hands in his. "They're frozen. I'll give you moxibustion. I have my kit with me."

"You're not listening," I said.

"Oh Deborah," he said. His face was close to mine. His breath warm. We stood nose to nose like horses, breathing each other's scent in. "You look so pale. They might have killed you."

"I got pregnant the night before you went to India."

"I'm calling the police. I'm taking you to the hospital." He led me by the hand to the pay telephone. He put a coin in. He didn't bother to knock off the chef's hat of snow. It had gotten higher.

"I didn't tell you earlier because I didn't know myself," I said.

"Be quiet. I'm trying to dial."

"You're not listening," I said and then I realized he was. He was listening, but he didn't want to remember. Like me, he didn't want to remember. I could see it in the way he picked up the phone. In the deliberate way he dialed, as if it required all his concentration. But I couldn't stop myself. I was hurting all over. I couldn't stop myself from making him remember, no more than I could stop me. "I got pregnant," I said. "It was a girl. I don't know how I know that but I do."

He put down the phone. "You're not pregnant," he said.

"No," I said. "Not anymore."

He jammed his hands in his pockets. He looked sad and frightened. It was unbearable.

I said, "Will it ever stop snowing?"

He tipped his face up to the sky, and for a moment I thought he was going to stick out his tongue, as I had done when a child, to catch the flakes. But he didn't. He just said, "I don't know."

I heard the sound of scraping then. Of a shovel on concrete. A familiar sound from my childhood. It might be my father, bald head protected by his favorite Russian-style hat that he thought made him look like a Cossack, slinging snow to the side of the driveway with his shovel, a wide-bodied model that was almost too heavy, when loaded with snow, for me to lift. He always began at the top of the driveway, plunging his shovel in the first drift with a vigor that remained unabated until he reached the bottom, while I followed behind, pushing my smaller shovel in the track he had made to make the edges neater. We worked steadily, without talking, while the resident blue jay in the sugar maple tree shrilly scolded us and the cardinal, a red male with whom the blue jay kept an uneasy territorial truce, took advantage of his opponent's distraction and flew with his duller colored mate to the bird feeder in the back yard. There they gorged on sunflower seeds to the delight of my watching sisters and then flitted, content and sated, amongst the lilac bushes that had grown as big as trees. I loved to shovel. I loved to be outside, where the snow made everything sparkle. I had not asked my mother if it was snowing in Cleveland, but it was always snowing in Cleveland. "Where are you going?" Sachio kept saying as he followed me to Aoyama dori. I looked all around for the tall figure of my father with the flaps of his hat turned up above his ears and his face red from exertion, but of course he wasn't there. The shovelers were city workers, dozens of them, short, slim men in dark uniforms. A chorus of shovelers, scraping their shovels on concrete.

I wanted to help them. They wouldn't let me. I knew this, without asking. It wasn't my place. I was superfluous in Tokyo. A bystander. I felt horribly homesick. The lump had gotten bigger. Twice in size. Maybe three times. Sachio always said I liked to exaggerate but it was as big as my chest. It filled it, squeezing my heart. I was sure my organs were being squeezed too. A pair of whirring trucks, glossy as the garbage containers, sucked up snow and then flung it backwards, into their beds, like elephants scooping up water and reaching behind with their trunks to spray themselves, like the elephants at Periyar Wildlife Sanctuary in India. I had stood on the opposite bank of the river, watching them for hours. I hadn't felt useless then. I hadn't thought of myself at all. I'd been engrossed in watching the elephants stamping their feet in the water, blowing it onto their backs, flapping their long ears. Now all I could do was watch the shovelers, and the trucks, and a lone taxi, which moved infinitely slowly, creeping behind the trucks, its windshield wipers sweeping back and forth. It was midnight black. It might be a hearse.

Sachio grasped my hand. He held on to me as if to prevent me from escaping and said, "We'll take that taxi to the hospital."

The taxi obediently came to a halt. Its pneumatic doors swished open. An old man got out of the taxi, followed by an old woman.

"I'm not going to the hospital," I said.

"Yes you are."

But I had already twisted out of his grasp and was plowing through the snow towards Mr. Ono and Mrs. Koyama. Mrs. Koyama looked much better than she had before. Almost hearty. But Mr. Ono looked frail. He looked as though he'd aged ten years. He stared at me as if he didn't know who I was. Tears spilled out of his eyes. I thought it was the cold until Mrs. Koyama smacked the hood of the taxi and said, when the taxi driver came out, "Take this gaijin to the hospital. She's been in a fight."

Sachio told me to get in the taxi, then exchanged a flurry of words with Mrs. Koyama. I couldn't understand their Japanese. It seemed to be a private code. I'd abandoned Mr. Ono once. I wasn't going to do it again. "I'm going to help you," I said to him. His eyes glittered. A lens was missing from his spectacles. He had been a Morse code operator in the Imperial Army. He'd learned Morse code in three months. Had to. They beat it into him. Boxed his ears when he'd made mistakes. They were cruel to him. Mrs. Koyama held his arm. She told him that they'd be home soon. She spoke to him lovingly, as if to a hurt child. She coaxed him away from me. I said, "He can't walk in this." I said, "It's too cold for him." I said, "Why doesn't he recognize me?"

"He doesn't have far to go," Sachio said. "He'll be home soon."

"What home?" I said as Sachio urged me to get into the taxi. "The yakuza said we have to move in a week. Where is he going to go? Where is he going to go at his age?"

"His wife will help him. Deborah, get in the taxi."

"That's not his wife. His wife died years ago and he never mentioned any children."

"He'll be all right. Get in, Deborah." He put his arm around me. I shrugged it off.

"How do the yakuza have the power to do that to us? Just kick us out like that."

"They were hired by someone with a lot of money who wants more."

"What good is Respect for the Aged Day? What good is that damn holiday? Why does the government even have it if they don't protect old people from being thrown out of their homes? It's a joke. He's too old to start over in a new neighborhood even if he can afford five months of rent to move."

Once Mr. Ono had clicked out Morse code for me on his kotatsu, using a pair of chopsticks. Like George Szell, beating out the time for his players. "What did you just type out?" I'd asked him. "The Americans are coming," he'd replied and we'd both laughed. We'd been drinking miso soup he'd made with red miso. Little clams floated in it, their shells open.

"There's nothing you can do," Sachio said. "Old Tokyo is vanishing."

"Why? What are they replacing it with? And how is it better? I want to know!"

"We have to go to the hospital. Please, Debby."

He let go of my hand. I hadn't even realized he'd been holding it. I looked at him through the thickening snow, through a haze of fatigue. Through a snow dream, and I was crying. He might have been, too.

I watched Mr. Ono from the taxi window. I watched him as long as I could. He leaned against Mrs. Koyama. They walked infinitely slowly.

At the hospital a nurse brought a wheelchair. She had smooth black hair and a smooth serene face. She pushed me down the hall and into a room and drew back the covers. I slipped into the casing of the sheets, the pod of the bed. It held me like a seed. Nothing happened, I told the doctor when he came and asked me how I had gotten so bruised. Nothing happened. But Sachio told the doctor about turning the corner and seeing three yakuza jump off of me. I thought at first they'd killed her, he said and the doctor said no she's just bruised. Dehydrated. Slightly incoherent.

It was two, I said. Little Bear didn't join in. I obstinately spoke in English, and the doctor didn't understand me that well and Sachio, who could speak English well, didn't understand me at all. Maybe he had been pretending to understand me all along.

It was two, I repeated. I could see them clearly from the top of the mountain.

What mountain? they asked me.

I said I didn't know because I hadn't actually climbed it. I found myself on top of it, just like that. If it could always be that easy to climb mountains, I told the doctor. We've climbed Yarigatake and Yatsugatake and Mt. Fuji and each time we shed sweat and tears. At least I did. Sachio flew up. He has strong legs. He always has to stop and wait for me, or did until he broke one of them.

"I didn't break my leg, you did," Sachio said. "It's long since healed."

I asked the doctor when I could go home and he said soon. He said he was going to give me something for the pain and I said I'm not in pain.

That wasn't strictly true. I felt pain, though the person feeling the pain hadn't been me. I wasn't the person getting beaten up at all. Whoever that was, was just a shell, a husk. She wasn't me. All along, she hadn't been me. She was someone else. She looked like me. She acted somewhat like me. She tried to fit in. She spoke decent Japanese.

Sachio said, "You're not going back there," and I thought he was speaking of the person I'd created, that shell, that husk. I thought he said that I wasn't going back to her, and I agreed. I slept for a while. The nurse put compresses on my face. I told her about the miscarriage.

Later, they did a D and C, to make sure nothing would fester inside and rot. They proved the yakuza wrong. Now I was clean. Emptied out.

The bed was warm. The room was warm. The nurses smiled at me kindly. There were three other patients in the room. We all had curtains around our bed. I stayed behind my curtain, while the other patients stayed behind theirs. We were like the court women in *The Tale of Genji*, shielded by our screens. Too shy to look out at the beautiful Genji, or forbidden to by custom. Sachio sat by my bed, as he had sat by his mother's. He kept watch. I slept, but didn't dream.

I started feeling better. I talked to Sachio in English. I kept my voice low, so my curtained neighbors wouldn't hear. I asked him to go back to the apartment. I asked him to find out how Mr. Ono and Mrs. Koyama were. I asked him to feed Brownie. He said, "I can't leave you." Then turned his back to me and started rummaging in his backpack.

"But you are leaving. You're going back to India."

He had his head down and was taking things out of his backpack. My things always got jumbled in my backpack, to his irritation. It's one big space, I used to say to him when we were packing for our camping trips. How do you get things to stay so neat?

"I'm not going back to India," he said.

"Why not? What's changed?"

He kept silent. I had always thought his silence a permanent condition.

"What are we going to do? Are we just going to live like we were? Fighting all the time? What kind of relationship is that?"

The bed next to mine creaked. I heard shuffling. Someone walking in their slippers. I had not even glimpsed this neighbor, but I didn't open the curtains now. She must be going to the bathroom. It was down the hall. She must not be that ill. We were in the room for patients who weren't seriously ill. Only resting.

"There's no reason for you to stay with me," I said.

"You mean you don't want me to?"

"I don't know," I said. "I'm confused."

He drew out a small box from deep within his backpack. "I got this for you."

It was a silver necklace, heavy, beautiful, with a matching bracelet. The kind of necklace you wore with a sari. I didn't know what to say. He was leaving me. He had come back to pack up his things, but he had brought me a present. I didn't understand anything.

I left that evening. I waited until Sachio had gone out to get dinner. I wrote him a note, much longer than the one I had written on the napkin, then put on my clothes. I fastened the necklace. I put on the bracelet and walked through the hallways. Nobody stopped me. I told them not to try. Outside, the snow leaked violet from a frosty sky, and on the huge screen TVs in the train stations I passed through, commentators discussed the dire consequences of a lengthening blizzard. But the trains were running. There were people on them, swaddled in warm clothes. Their somber faces steadied me. The neon lights blazed, and in the smoke-filled Go clubs whose windows crowded close to the Yamanote Line train in some places, the Go players bent over their boards, moving pieces. I headed home to Brownie.

At Shin Aoyama station, workers mopped melting snow. Teenagers leapt over puddles. The shovelers were still at work on Aoyama dori, and I walked on one of the paths they had made until I turned onto the little alley that led to the apartment building. The falling snow began to thin until finally only a few flakes twirled down, white-gold and lonely, and that's when I remembered that Mr. Ono had told me, not long after I moved in, that a maple tree had once grown in front of the apartment building, shedding scarlet leaves, glorious and vibrant, in autumn. It had long ago been cut down. Not even a stump remained. I didn't know what would happen to any of us.

Tokyo Pleasureland

When the waitress set down the bowl of cold yellow noodles in front of Mr. Sato, he immediately slid the bowl over to me, a display of Western gallantry so surprising to the waitress that she froze and stared at Mr. Sato as if she didn't know what other odd things he might do.

"Thank you," I said. I was surprised, too.

"You're the first foreigner I've ever talked to," Mr. Sato said, as he had said earlier that day, when we'd first met under a ginkgo tree. "How well you speak Japanese."

"Thank you," I said again.

A tremor passed through the waitress, a slight shaking that reminded me of the way cows shake off flies by making their skin quiver without seeming to move the muscles underneath. Then she bustled away and soon returned with a second bowl of hiyashi chuka for Mr. Sato, adorned with slivers of cucumber, strips of pork, and eggs fried into a roll and sliced thin. The Japanese were masters at slicing thin. In the days when I had gone hiking in the Chichibu Mountains, I had always eaten my carrots out of sight of the other hikers so that they couldn't see how thickly I had cut them. "Like pencil stubs," my Japanese husband used to say. We had long since moved to the U.S. and divorced, after which he had converted to Catholicism and married a dancer, presumably a Catholic, since an unctuous secretary from the Archdiocese of Seattle had called me to verify that I was Jewish so our marriage could be annulled and my ex could slice carrots for his dancing wife without sin.

"Eat up," Mr. Sato said. He vigorously stirred hot mustard into his sauce with the tips of his chopsticks, and slurped up noodles. I picked up my own chopsticks and dug in.

I had met Mr. Sato, eighty-six years old, widowed now for twenty years, on the grounds of Asakusa Kannon Temple when I had moved out of the sun and into the shade of a gingko tree under which Mr. Sato was sitting, his orange bike parked beside him, fanning himself with a fan, the cheap kind that did not fold up but was made of cardboard and stood stiffly open. Despite the August heat the temple swarmed with foreign tourists, young white women in shorts and halter tops speaking French to young white men in shorts and T-shirts, sunburned American tourists with large paunches pointing digital cameras at everything, Russian-speaking families trying on yukattas in a shop which displayed a sign in English stating "we carry extra-large sizes." The men's soccer team of Oman was sitting on the steps of the temple, their long legs stretched out in front of them, talking in I knew not what language, though I knew it was not called Omanese. A doughy young man who turned out to be from Sweden and who seemed lonely had begun telling me about himself as I was tossing coins into the wooden box in front of the temple altar. He was still talking when we sat down next to Mr. Sato, whose name we did not yet know. By this time the young man had introduced himself as Daniel, told me that he composed electronic music and was twenty-five years old, and that while living in Taiwan prior to moving to Japan he had dated an older woman. "I like older women," he said just before we sat down under the tree.

"What happened to her?" I asked to be polite. I had been raised to be polite. This sometimes led men to talk to me longer than I wanted them to.

"She broke up with me," Daniel said. He rubbed sweat off his forehead with a plump, pale hand. There were specks of moisture on his glasses. "She was a singer," he said.

The old man sat ramrod straight on the other side of me, fanning himself rhythmically though he looked cool in light blue slacks belted at his narrow waist and a spotless white shirt. Two plastic bags lay in the front basket of his orange bicycle. The old man obviously lived in the neighborhood. He must have gone out shopping, then stopped to rest under the shade of the tree. I suddenly remembered that after throwing coins into the wooden box in front of the temple I had not clapped my hands together three times to call the spirits to attention, as was customary, because Daniel had interrupted my performance of the ritual. "Do you know what kind of temple this is?" he had asked, but had not shown even a cursory interest in my reply, soon launching into a recitation of his life story without asking me anything about myself but my name.

"She was supposed to meet me for dinner one night but she never showed up," Daniel said. What had his ex-girlfriend seen in him in the first place? Everything about him was pale, his hair, his eyes, his sweaty arms, the rims of his glasses. He looked like he ate too much candy and never exercised. He looked like he could comfortably sit next to me for several hours at least. I sighed, but Daniel didn't seem to notice. In front of the temple, an old woman lit a stick of incense and stuck it into the ash at the center of a huge ceramic urn. She cupped her hands in the smoke as if trying to embrace it, then waved the smoke towards her knees. If Daniel asked me what the old woman was doing, I would say that she, along with everyone standing around the urn, had come to the temple to light incense, dip their hands in the smoke and then touch the parts of their body that needed healing: a stiff neck, a bad back, a bum knee. A young man bent over at the waist while his girlfriend, laughing, tried to direct the smoke to his head, then rapped on his skull with her knuckles. An old man dipped his hand in the smoke as if dipping it in water, then clapped his hand to his heart. Maybe he feared his heart was giving out. Maybe it was broken. Clap, clap, clap. Like a soldier giving a salute. When Daniel had started speaking to me, I had been about to clap my hands in front of the altar for my father-in-law's spirit, even though I didn't know if I believed in spirits. "I believe in it all," my best friend Linda used to say. On bean-throwing day in February, Linda had always stood in the doorway of her house, throwing beans over her shoulders and chanting, "Oni wo soto, fuku wo uchi." "Devil go out, happiness come in." On the last day I'd seen my father-in-law before leaving Japan fifteen years ago, he had kicked up into a handstand next to me at the wall as if he did it every day and, after coming down, hadn't been breathless in the least.

"When I called her she told me she didn't want to see me again," Daniel was saying now, about his ex-girlfriend. "She wouldn't tell me why. She just said it was over."

"That was mean of her," I said, and meant it. A picture flashed into my mind of my ex sticking out his tongue at me. I even had a photograph of him doing it. Now he stuck his tongue out at a priest every Sunday when he walked up to the front of the church to get a communion wafer. That would be a sight to see but it wasn't one I ever would see, which was why on impulse I had purchased a ticket to Japan, where we had lived, and where, every morning, he had prayed to his mother's spirit at the Buddhist altar in our apartment, which he kept well-polished and heaped with persimmons when in season. Out of season he piled up apples, but persimmons had been his mother's favorite fruit. "Are you sure you want to go in August?" the travel agent in the U.S., a young woman named Eriko Shiotani, had said. "It's hot and humid in August." *Taihen* hot and humid, was what she'd actually said to the dismay of a coworker sitting at the next desk, who had shot her a warning look. I replied that I especially wanted to go in August. I had said that I didn't mind the heat.

"I've heard Japanese women are nice," Daniel said, adding, confidently, "I'm going to get a Japanese girlfriend soon."

"You'd be better off talking to a Japanese woman if you want to get a Japanese girlfriend," I almost blurted out. I had once been as talkative as Daniel; I'd confessed things, though only to Sachio and later to Linda; I'd spilled my guts with ease.

"When I get a girlfriend, I'll buy a scooter," Daniel said. "I'll take my girlfriend for rides around Tokyo."

A branch of the gingko tree shading us swayed in the hot breeze, letting a ray of sunlight through to blind me, and I scooted an inch over on the bench, towards the old man, who promptly scooted a little further over himself. I had been through this routine many times on the train. Whenever you sat down next to a Japanese they always shifted slightly, even if it was rush hour and they were packed in thigh to thigh, with nowhere to move. Somehow they moved, if only a milliliter. They made room.

"It's hot, isn't it," I remarked to the old man in Japanese.

He brightened up. "That it is! Very hot! Too hot for human beings!"

He turned his fan around so that he was holding the wide end and presented it to me handle first.

"Oh thank you but I couldn't."

"Take it please!" the old man insisted.

On one side of the fan, *Tokyo Pleasureland* was written in large black letters, in English. Party balloons and exploding firecrackers had been painted on the other side, along with the black silhouettes of two women in kimono, wearing wooden geta and pictured as dancing. I wondered where "Tokyo Pleasureland" was, what the old man had done there. It was probably one of those Shinjuku bars where women flirted with men and poured them drinks. I fanned myself. I fanned my neck and face. It helped. I felt a little cooler.

"I'm sorry I don't have a fan for your husband." The old man leaned forward to peer around me at Daniel. The two men smiled and nodded at each other.

"He's not my husband," I said.

The old man looked carefully at me, and then at Daniel. "Is he your son then?"

I hid a smile behind the fan. "No. He just started talking to me a few minutes ago."

"He talks well," the old man observed. "Can he speak Japanese?"

"I don't think so."

"But you speak Japanese. Good Japanese."

"It's rusty. I used to live here but this is the first time I've been back in fifteen years."

"What are you talking about?" Daniel asked. "What's he saying?"

"He's complimenting me on my Japanese."

"I wish I could speak Japanese. When I get a Japanese girlfriend, she'll teach it to me."

The sun climbed higher, but the leaves of the gingko tree shading us looked fresh and green despite the heat. Several sparrows took a dust bath near the roots of the tree, energetically flinging dust into the air with their wings.

"Are you American?" the old man asked, and then, when I said yes, remarked, "A lot of Americans come here but I've never talked to any before. You're the first."

"He said I'm the first American he's ever talked to," I translated for Daniel.

"I'm not American," Daniel said, pointing a thick forefinger at himself. "I'm Sweda-jin. Not America-jin. Sweda-jin."

"What did he say?" the old man asked.

"That he's Swedish."

"Sweda-jin!" the old man exclaimed.

"Sweda-jin," Daniel seconded. He smiled at the old man, showing white teeth.

A teenager wearing a black t-shirt that said *Run Around Naked* in English on it sauntered by us, slugging down a bottle of water and talking on his cell phone. A young couple kissed each other on the lips. Housewives bicycled by, each balancing one child on a seat at the back. The children were all dressed alike in summer kindergarten uniforms of dark blue, the girls in skirts, the boys in shorts, with round straw hats atop their heads, tied with beige ribbons under their chins. They were sleeping, their heads lolling to one side or another as their mothers, too busy talking to keep a stable course, unsteadily steered. One mother nearly missed hitting a statue of a squirrel, swerving at the last minute. Her little boy kept on sleeping, his head tilted to the side, his hat firmly secured.

"Do you have any children?" the old man asked.

"No."

"Does he?"

"I don't think so."

"Maybe you can have them together."

 I choked back a laugh. "I'm old enough to be his mother."

"You look young," the old man said. "Your stomach doesn't stick out, like the stomachs of most foreigners. You're slim, like my daughter." He added, matter-of-factly, "I haven't seen her for sixty years."

"That's a long time." Had he said six years and not sixty? It had been over six years since I'd seen or talked to my ex and I'd hesitated to call him, hesitated a long time. But in the end I had to know whether my father-in-law was alive or dead, and so I had looked up Sachio's phone number in Seattle, where he now lived.

"I'm going to Japan next week," I said after he picked up the phone. "Is your father still alive? Is he still living at home?"

"I don't want you to contact my family. I told you that when we divorced. You didn't listen."

"Can't you at least tell me whether he's alive or not?" I unwisely retorted, getting angrier with each breath I took. "He was my relative, too."

"Don't call me again." Sachio slammed down the phone.

"What a jerk," Linda had said when I called her to report on the conversation. "He could tell you if your father-in-law is still alive. That wouldn't be so hard to do." She was still married to her Japanese husband and lived with him and their three sons in a house in LA with a swimming pool.

So much had changed in the fifteen years since I'd lived in Tokyo, I'd tell her when I returned. Everyone talked on cell phones while waiting on the train platform, or while sitting in the Café Veloce in my old Saitama neighborhood, eating hotdogs, or tuna sandwiches, or coffee jelly topped with whipped cream. I had seen a bicyclist along the Ochiai River, leaning over his handlebars, punching a text message into his phone. He'd managed to stay upright. He hadn't fallen over or hit anything. But Linda would know about these changes. She visited her in-laws in Japan almost every year. "Maybe if there had been cell phones and e-mail when we lived in Japan," I'd tell her instead, "we wouldn't have felt so isolated from our family and friends in the States."

"I wish I could speak English," the old man was saying now. "So many foreigners come to this temple, but I can't say anything to them."

"They don't all speak English."

"All I can say is 'thank you.'"

"Why's he thanking you?" Daniel asked.

"It's the only English phrase he knows."

"Thank you," the old man said.

"You're welcome," Daniel said.

"During O-bon," I could have said to Eriko Shiotani when she sold me my ticket, "my father-in-law and I used to make horses out of eggplants for the spirits of the dead to ride back to earth on." Instead, I told her that I loved seeing the matsuri in August, everyone in costume, dancing. I told her I loved watching the August fireworks.

"The mosquitoes are very bad in August," was all she had said. But there were fireflies, too, and a black-crowned night heron with a slate blue back and two white plumes streaming from its head which flew down at dusk to stand on the banks of the Ochiai River. Almost every evening since I'd arrived in Japan I watched him, an intent and patient fisherman, until the dusk deepened and he could no longer be seen.

Pigeons pecked at the ground. A group of women holding lacy parasols to shade themselves from the blinding sun hurried across the pavement and up the wide temple steps. A woman in a polyester suit lifted a panting white toy poodle with a big pink bow around its neck out of her bicycle basket and carried it up the temple steps. She handed a camera to one of the parasol-holding women and posed for a picture with her dog. She was childless, I knew from the way she held her dog, the way she cuddled it while the camera clicked. Maybe, upon returning to America, I would get a dog, but I would never get a toy poodle, or adorn it with a pink bow. I would get a rough dog, a scrappy thing.

"Why did I bother calling Sachio in the first place?" I had said to Linda. "Otō-san was eighty-five years old when I left Japan. He'd be one hundred if he was still alive."

"You wanted to know."

"But he must not be alive any longer."

"The Japanese live a long time. I heard about a woman in Okinawa who's a hundred and fourteen years old."

"Isn't it troublesome for your parents that you left America and came to Japan?" Mr. Sato asked me. I didn't remember when, during the conversation, we had exchanged names. "Aren't they worried about you?"

"They were happy I got to come here after an absence of fifteen years." Daniel gave me a questioning look. "He's asking if my parents were worried about me coming here."

Daniel looked startled. "Why would they be?"

"It's a normal question for an older person to ask. Family relationships are different here."

"I had to leave Sweden. There were no jobs in my small city. Nothing to do. I was living at home."

"Lots of young people in Japan live with their parents, but I understand why you wanted to leave," I said to Daniel, and, to Mr. Sato, "He didn't have a job. He came here looking for work." And girls. He seems to be one of those foreign men who come here because they want an Asian woman. But I didn't say this. Maybe he just wanted a woman, period. He was, after all, twenty-five years old. He might end up going to places like Tokyo Pleasureland, paying women to pour him drinks. Or maybe he'd find a Japanese girlfriend. They'd have children together. They'd be happy.

"Atsui," Mr. Sato was saying while I hadn't been paying attention.

But Daniel was paying attention. "Atsui," he said. He fanned himself with his hand, as Mr. Sato was doing. "But tell him it's hotter in Taiwan," Daniel said. "Compared to a Taiwan summer, this is cool." He waited until I had translated this, then asked, "What's the Japanese word for 'cool'?"

"Suzushii."

"Sushi? Like the food?"

"No, suzushii."

"Suzushiku nai," Mr. Sato said and I laughed.

Passersby looked at us curiously. We were an odd threesome, an old Japanese man in perfectly ironed blue pants and a spotless white shirt, a middle-aged foreign woman in nondescript olive green pants, her graying hair cut boyishly short, and a pudgy blonde youth in black jeans and a black t-shirt. "Do you know what kind of temple this is?" Daniel had asked when he'd approached me at the altar.

"Buddhist. Kannon is the Goddess of Mercy. But you can't see her at the altar. They've hidden her image from view."

A young monk strode across the courtyard. Despite his black robes, he looked cool.

"I came here to pray every week during the war," Mr. Sato said. "I think that's why I survived the bombing of Tokyo. The temple didn't. It had to be rebuilt."

I looked at the temple, which was grand and painted mostly red and had wide steps leading up to it, upon which the long-limbed Oman men's soccer team sat, looking cool in their sweats despite the heat. The woman in polyester now sat on the temple steps, bouncing her poodle on her knee.

"My wife survived the bombing, too, but she's been dead now for twenty years."

"I'm sorry about the war," I said. "And the bombing. It was a terrible thing."

"What are you talking about?" Daniel asked.

"The firebombing of Tokyo. By the Americans. One hundred thousand people were killed."

"Like Dresden," Daniel said. "Before the war Swedish schoolchildren studied German as a second language, but afterwards we studied English. I'm glad because I'll be able to get a job here teaching English. I've heard that lots of foreign men meet Japanese girls that way." Daniel stared longingly at two young women walking by, heads bent close, giggling over something, both dressed fashionably in short skirts and high heels.

"My wife was from Niigata. She had the typical face of a woman from Niigata. Yours is long and thin." Mr. Sato grasped my arm above the elbow and gave it a squeeze. "This is the first time I've touched a foreign woman!" He released my arm and beamed.

"It's the same," I said. "We all have arms and legs."

So much had changed in the fifteen years since I'd lived in Tokyo, I'd tell Linda, but so much had not. Tokyo still had luxury shops and people wearing elegant clothes, though I'd also seen hundreds of homeless men camping in Shinjuku Park, and "One hundred yen" stores everywhere selling cheap goods. The salarymen still practiced their golf swings with their umbrellas and read newspapers which contained more photographs of women in bikinis than news. Housewives still rode their bicycles around their neighborhoods to shop, or take their children to school. There was an innocence, a graciousness which remained.

"The monks buried the statue of Kannon before the bombing," Mr. Sato said. "They buried it and it was saved."

"I can't decide which girl is prettier," Daniel said, shading his eyes with his hand, watching the young women crossing the courtyard on their high heels. "Do you think they're twins?"

The sun hung, heavy and orange, in the smoggy sky. The woman in polyester lowered her poodle into her bicycle basket, obviously preparing to leave. Sweat dripped down my back. I wiped my damp face with a handkerchief I'd remembered to stuff in my purse before leaving my room. I lifted my bangs and fanned my forehead.

"Would you like to get a cold drink?" Mr. Sato asked. "Would you like to get some food?"

"Mr. Sato wants to know if we'd like to get lunch," I said, but Daniel was still staring at the young women.

"Do you think those girls would talk to me?"

"Why not?" I resisted the impulse to add something sarcastic. I had always loved the politeness of the Japanese. "We're not Japanese," I knew Linda would say if she were here and not in LA with her family. "And do you call those men smoking in your face and pinching your butt well mannered?"

"Daniel's not going with us to lunch," I told Mr. Sato. "He wants to talk to those young women over there."

Mr. Sato's face fell. "Ah!" he exclaimed.

"He's disappointed," I said to Daniel. "He wants you to come with us and eat."

Mr. Sato mimed eating. "Gohan!" he said, but Daniel was giving us his apologies, tucking in his t-shirt, smoothing back his hair.

"He's the second foreigner I've ever talked to," Mr. Sato said after we'd stood up and said goodbye to Daniel, after we'd bowed and he'd walked away. I watched Daniel hurry towards the two women, now standing at the far end of the temple complex, at a cold drinks stand, sipping vivid blue iced drinks. I had been twenty-four years old when I met Sachio. My hair had been dark brown with no gray. "I don't feel comfortable with most foreigners," he had said. "But I feel comfortable with you."

"My daughter disappeared during the bombing," Mr. Sato said. "She was four years old. I was working at an army building outside of Tokyo and she and my wife were at home."

I struggled to console him, to find the right words. The young women lowered their drinks as Daniel approached, smiled with blue-tinged lips. What were they drinking? It was such a startling blue. I was glad that I didn't have to translate what Mr. Sato was saying to Daniel, who only cared about pursuing girls.

"People ran to the Sumida River. They ran and jumped in to escape the flames. My wife carried our daughter to the river. It's just over there." He pointed in the direction where the two women were standing. He took his hat off the seat of his bicycle and put it on his head. "They got separated. There were so many people running, pushing. For years, I wondered if my daughter had survived. If she was still alive."

An image came to me of his daughter, a heart-shaped face and black hair.

"Maybe she was," I said. "Is," I corrected myself.

"It was March," Mr. Sato said. "The Sumida River was very cold." He poked the fan, resting in my lap. "You're not fanning yourself. Please do." He stepped out of the shade of the tree, into the heat. "Have you ever eaten hiyashi chuka?" he said. "Do you like Japanese food?" He kicked up the kickstand on his orange bicycle and it reminded me of my father-in-law, whose bicycle, I remembered, had been green. It might be my father-in-law I was following behind on one of the crowded streets that radiated from the temple compound like the spokes of a wheel. He had served in Malaysia with the Japanese army during the war, marched in the jungle. He hadn't talked about what he'd done or seen, only about the monkey he'd found, and made a pet of, and fed scraps of food. He fed all the stray cats in his neighborhood. Whenever we visited Shizuoka, he fed me, fed my husband, cooked us the choicest food. Perhaps he cooked for his new daughter-in-law when she visited with Sachio from Seattle. Perhaps he was still alive, and that's why I had not clapped even one clap for his spirit at the temple altar, why Daniel had interrupted me before I could begin.

Haiku

She closed the book, placed it on the table, and finally decided to walk through the door. She said good morning in Japanese to the man waiting beside the stretcher, and his smile and deep bow eased her fear. She lay on the stretcher and he pushed it down the hallway. She had begged the nurse not to let anyone wheel it into her room. "I want to go out to it," she had said. "I don't want it to come to me."

The man had thick black hair touched with gray at the temples. Romance gray, the Japanese called it. Her own hair, once near enough to black that the Japanese sometimes mistook her for one of their own, had turned solidly gray except for a darker patch on the crown. "That's where the tumor is, right?" she had joked with Mori-senséi, her English-speaking oncologist. "X marks the spot." Mori-senséi went on talking about surgery and skull drilling. He'd fired radiation at her head several weeks before and wanted to do it again but she refused.

If she had brought her book she would hold it up above her, squinting at the haiku she'd been reading when the stretcher arrived. Better yet the book would float above her, at a distance further than her arms could reach so that, without her reading glasses, she could make out the words. Picking up speed, the man pushed her around a corner with a squeak of the wheels and to her surprise something—the sound?—dislodged the haiku from her tumor-addled memory. She recited it aloud and only when the man abruptly stopped pushing did she realize she'd recited it in Japanese.

"He came to a dead stop," she tried to joke with Mori-senséi after the stretcher later delivered her to his pristine operating room. "He asked me, 'How do you know that haiku?'"

She recited the haiku for the man once more with as much feeling as she could while he mouthed the words:

Kokoro kara
yuki utsukushi ya
nishi no kumo

They were blocking the hall. And yet nurses and doctors and patients and relatives of patients streamed easily around them and she thought that the ghosts of the dead might be streaming around them, too. Women with hair like seaweed and phosphorescent skin. On the news last night, she watched helicopters dumping water on burning power plants and cars floating out to sea. "No more radiation," she had told Mori-senséi. "I just want to sit in a quiet room and read poetry. I used to read long books, but now I can only read a sprinkling of words." He sent the stretcher for her anyway. He said surgery might buy her a year.

"Of all Issho's haiku, my mother loved that one best," the man said. "She wrote it in calligraphy on a scroll I hung over her altar." His eyes shone with memories. "How do you know it?"

"I was reading it before you came. Maybe I don't have cancer after all. Maybe the doctor is wrong because I can even remember the English translation."

From deep in my heart
how beautiful the snow
clouds in the west.

"Thank you!" the man exclaimed. "My English is very poor, but how tender that sounds!" Starry tears lit up his eyes but he resumed pushing her down the hallway because he had to. They soon arrived at the operating room.

The Grocery Store Cart

Michiko pushed the grocery cart down the aisle, marveling at how it was so large you could put a dead body in it. She peered at the strange packages on the shelves, sounding out unfamiliar English words on the labels and trying to decide what she could choose that was both edible and would take up space in the cart. She lingered in front of Skip-py, wondering if the brown stuff in the jar was some kind of dog food and thinking of her little dog Poppy, who had nipped her for the very first time before she'd left Japan, and when she turned around her father was lying in the cart, dressed in his pajamas and robe, as he had been when she'd found him lying outside the door to the family bath. His English was excellent and he spoke to her in it now, from the dead, as it were, and this is what he said, or at least what she thought he said, as her own English was much poorer than his, an old rattling train compared to his bullet train express. He spoke fast. As she leaned over the cart to listen, she saw a little girl, being wheeled by her mother, gaping at him with an open mouth and a tongue that hung out like a dog's.

"Close your mouth," the child's mother said. "You're going to catch a fly."

"Michiko-chan," her father said after he waved at the little girl, and the girl waved back. "You didn't give Watanabe a chance. How can you judge a man by his dislike of the food you cooked? Cook him something better!" Her father paused, and looking up at her from behind the specta-cles that were always sliding down his nose but were not sliding now, he said, "Try making him an American meal. There's a whole store of food here. Shop my child!"

Michiko hung her head down. Her father had arranged for her to meet Watanabe with the thought they'd make a good match, and Michiko had tried to like Watanabe. Tried hard. She told her father this but he only said "Sh! People are listening! It's not good to have a private conversation here," and then he fell silent, and shut his eyes, and looked so dead that she feared he'd never come back to life. What's worse, she had to put the jar of Skip-py in the cart, and where would she put it? On his chest? He fit perfectly into the cart, every part of him, like azuki bean sweets in a sweet box.

"Father!" Michiko cried out but he didn't respond, and it was all Michiko could do not to shake him, as she'd done when she'd found him slumped outside the door to the bath, his spectacles on (he had the bad habit of reading in the bath), his face flushed, as he'd liked his bath water scalding hot. She pushed his shoulder with one finger, as she'd seen a large American woman do to a package of meat, but he batted at her hand. Michiko was so disconcerted that she walked away from him, only stopping when something golden in a bin caught her eye. She ran back with it to the cart and tossed it in and when she dared to look, her father was holding a pineapple in his arms. He patted its bristly head and said, "Did you dislike Watanabe because he was going bald?"

"No!" Michiko said indignantly, though it was true, Watanabe had an unprepossessing appearance and a woman liked some dash in a man. She had not asked what Watanabe looked like when her father first informed her he was trying to arrange a match, fantasizing that Watanabe was a broad-shouldered, well-muscled man who would bestow passionate kisses on her lips, like the heroes in the Harlequin romances she read, which were translated into Japanese by a friend who had divorced her businessman husband after finding a note from a woman in his pants. But Watanabe had been short and balding, with a little pot belly. Due to either nerves or allergies, he sniffed a lot. They had gone to Aoyama cemetery at the peak of cherry blossom season, when the branches hung with plump pink and white blooms, but Watanabe, oblivious to their swollen beauty, had hurried her towards Aoyama fire station just outside the cemetery grounds, where he gazed admiringly at the shiny red fire engine parked outside. He loved motor vehicles. He talked about them a lot.

"Excuse me," a woman said from behind Michiko.

"I'm sorry!" Michiko saw that she was blocking the aisle, and pushed her cart to the side.

"What are you going to do with that pineapple?" the woman asked as she pushed her own cart by.

"Cook it with ham," Michiko's father replied.

The woman waited for Michiko to answer. She didn't seem to see Michiko's father in the cart.

"Do you speak English?" the woman asked. "Where are you from?"

"Japan."

"This is a nice juicy ripe fruit," Michiko's father said. He gave the pineapple a squeeze. "You don't see many of these in Japan." He patted the stiff leaves atop its head, as he had rarely patted Poppy, who, he claimed despite evidence to the contrary, was a flea-ridden dog. Poppy had started barking after Michiko found her father outside the bath and didn't stop until a veterinarian in Kichijoji plunged a tranquilizer into her rump, knocking her out for twenty-four hours. She woke up a different dog.

"I've never bought a fresh pineapple before," the woman said. "Only canned. Are they hard to peel?"

Michiko didn't know what "hard to peel" meant. "Yes," she said.

Her father had always told her that she had a good ear for English, but that she didn't understand the meaning of half of what she heard. "You don't study hard enough," her father used to say, but now he didn't say anything at all. He had a blissful look on his face, as if lying on his futon instead of in a grocery cart. He looked as if he lay in carts, holding pineapples, all the time.

"I suppose I should be more adventurous in my diet," the woman said. She turned and grabbed a package of meat from her cart, the same package, Michiko realized, and the same large woman who had earlier poked it. "Tonight I'm going to cook Sloppy Joes. My mother loves them. She's ninety years old but she's reverting to her childhood. She gums her food, but she can still chow down a Sloppy Joes. It just takes her a while."

"I had my teeth right until the end," Michiko's father said. "I died with all my teeth in my mouth. The last meal I had was buckwheat noo-dles but it could have been something harder to chew and I would have been all right. I could probably bite through this pineapple. Especially," he sniffed its round bottom, "because it's ripe."

"My mother lives in the past," the woman said. "She thinks my father is still alive. You know, if that pineapple were smaller it would look a lot like a grenade, but then if I were smaller I'd look like Raquel Welch."

"Do you ladies need help?" a store clerk suddenly asked. "Are you finding everything all right?"

"She might need help finding something to eat with that pineapple," the woman said, nodding at Michiko.

"Margaret cooked pineapples with ham," Michiko's father said.

"Holler if you need help," the clerk said. "Have a nice day!" He straightened some things on a shelf, then strode off.

"Who's Margaret?" Michiko asked her father, but he didn't reply. A month before he'd died she'd overheard him talking and at first she'd thought he was talking to himself.

"Margaret," he said, "why did you die before I saw you one last time?"

Michiko had peeked through a gap in the sliding door at her father, squatting in front of Poppy, who was looking at him with her ears pitched forwards, her eyes intent on something he held in his hand. A piece of pork. A piece of Chinese-style pork, simmered for four hours in a broth flavored with ginger root and green onions and then sliced thin and served with hot mustard sauce. Michiko knew this because she'd made the pork herself. Her father loved her Chinese pork. But he was feeding it to the dog, who, the vet said, needed to be walked more and put on a diet. "See this?" the vet had said, squeezing Poppy's freckled, paunchy belly. "That's fat." Michiko waited for Poppy to bite the vet. She had wanted to bite him herself. "Father!" she almost cried out, but her father looked so happy squatting there, as he had sometimes done with Michiko as a child when they were waiting for the bus to take them to Mother, squatting comfortably and holding out the succulent pork to Poppy, who wolfed it down with grunts of pleasure.

"You've been holding that jar of peanut butter a long time," the woman said. "May I?"

Michiko handed her the jar.

"Chunky salted. My father ate it with strawberry jam." The woman put the jar in her own cart. Michiko didn't ask for it back. Perhaps the woman's father was lying there, holding the jar of peanut butter. Perhaps everyone in the store was wheeling around someone dead in their carts. She was sorry she had fled the sight of her father's calligraphy brushes, lined up on a table in his empty bedroom next to the little black ink pot from which the ink was fast evaporating. She wanted to return to their house in Japan.

"How do you say 'peanut butter' in Japanese?" the woman asked. "Don't be tongue tied. I talk a lot, believe me, I know. I can even talk in the dentist's chair with his instruments in my mouth."

After Michiko's father had died, after his ashes and bones were in the urn, after Poppy had been tranquilized and then revived with seemingly no interest in ever again sitting in Michiko's lap, Michiko had done the boldest thing ever in her life. She called Watanabe. When he answered, she almost hung up out of shyness and fright but finally gasped out her name and asked if he might be so kind as to meet her if he had time. Watanabe sounded wary, and surprised, and at first she was sure he would refuse, as she had refused his invitations over the months, that he would even hang up. But in the end he'd stammered out a yes, and she'd soon found herself sitting across from him in Anna Miller's pie shop in Aoyama, where he'd eaten two slices of banana cream pie and talked, to her surprise, rather easily to her about movies she liked. After-wards they'd strolled around looking into shop windows at the kimonos, the carved hair ornaments, the designer shoes that could not, Michiko was sure, fit any mortal's feet. "I'm very sorry about your father," he finally said as they were eyeing a row of cakes frosted with pink roses in a bakery window. She burst out crying. He'd sniffed as if about to cry too, then pressed a handkerchief in her hand.

"Larry said I could have been a ventriloquist," the woman said. "He's not my dentist, he's my boyfriend."

Michiko's father appeared to be dozing. The pineapple rested against the side of his head, its bottom in the hollow of his neck.

"It's hard for a man to be with a woman who's taking care of her elderly mother. It's not like we have much privacy, or time."

"I . . ." Michiko began, but the woman went on, "We only get away once a week, when the respite worker comes. We go shopping. But half the time Larry sits in the car reading *Auto Racing* magazine."

"Her boyfriend likes cars," Michiko's father said sleepily.

"He isn't my boyfriend," Michiko said.

"You have a boyfriend?" the woman asked.

"Yes," Michiko said. "I mean no."

"I understand. It's an on and off romance. Sometimes I get upset with Larry for staying in the car but he says it's boring for him in the store because I gab with every soul in sight. Wait until I tell him I met someone from Japan. He'll be sorry he didn't come with me inside."

"I took care of my father," Michiko said, but the woman interrupted again. "Can you say something in Japanese? I'd love to hear you say something in Japanese."

Michiko's face felt hot. She hated how her emotions flamed up, how embarrassed she got.

"Go on," the woman urged her. "Don't be shy."

"Hattori-san dō omou?" The line, from a movie, but which one? It had just sprung out of her mouth.

The woman's face lit up. "Isn't that something!" she said. "Isn't that something else!"

Michiko could see the pretty girl this woman had once been shining from her fleshy face. She could see her hunger, her eagerness for life, and where had her own gone? She leaned over her father. "Who's Margaret, father? Tell me. I want to know."

"You met her. You were seven. I took you to New York. You said Margaret was pretty. You held her hand."

"No I did not," Michiko said.

"I talk to myself all the time," the woman said. "That's why I keep busy filling up my grocery cart. I fill it with boxes of crackers and macaroni and cheese and Cap'n Crunch cereal, which I don't even like that much. I hide the diapers for my mother under everything else." She leaned over her cart and started moving things around.

"My father liked to speak English," Michiko said. "He preferred it to his mother tongue. I never asked him why he liked English so much." Even though she was staying nearby, with a college roommate who had immigrated to Oregon, she wouldn't come to this store again, but then she didn't know how she could leave her father lying in the cart. If only somebody saw him and screamed in surprise. If only somebody said there's a man wearing spectacles and a bathrobe lying in your cart. But people walked by without looking at Michiko's father, or at Michiko. They didn't notice her. She had not been noticed, except by Watanabe-san, who had looked stricken when she'd told him she was leaving Japan for a long time.

"Sometimes I feel like I'm burying my mother," the woman said. "I feel like I'm smothering her under all these things in my cart. The truth is, I'm tired of taking care of her. Sometimes I'm just so tired that I want her to die. Is that a bad thing? Am I a bad daughter?"

"Hattori-san dō omou?" Michiko said. "That's what the father said to his daughter in that movie. It means, 'Do you like Mr. Hattori?' But it didn't matter, because Mr. Hattori was already engaged to somebody else. My father knew all the lines from Ozu's films very well. I think he wanted to be a movie director. He didn't want to be a museum director at all."

"That's how I met Margaret," Michiko's father interrupted. "She was sitting in front of me at the New York Film Festival, eating popcorn. She had red hair in a bun this high." He waved his fingers over the pineapple. "I couldn't see the screen. Instead of watching the movie, I watched her big hair, even when the screen got dark."

"Larry loves the movies," the woman said. "His favorite is *Bonnie and Clyde.*"

"Beautiful hair," Michiko's father said. "Her pride and joy. As you are mine."

Michiko wasn't sure exactly what her father had said. Something good. He had said something good about her; he had bestowed rare praise. But now he just looked tired. His dreamy look had been replaced by a weary one, as if death were wearing him out. The pineapple slipped from beneath his chin and rolled into the crook of his arm.

"I cooked for my father," Michiko said. "He liked pork. Some Japanese don't like meat, but he liked it too much." She bent over the cart but couldn't bear to touch her father again. Her mother had been ill. She saw things nobody else saw, talked to people nobody else could see. Michiko and her father had gone to visit her, together, when Michiko was a child.

Her father always whispered in his wife's ear. "I miss you," he must have said. "Come home. We're waiting. I miss you so much." Michiko tried to lift the pineapple, but it remained in her father's arms.

"Take this ham," the woman said, lifting a hunk of meat from her cart and holding it out. "That pineapple looks lonely by itself."

"Thank you but I can't," Michiko said.

"Take it. Please. I'm just remembering that Elvis liked pineapple. How could I forget? With marshmallows and maraschino cherries. You can give your father that, but for now, feed him ham." The woman put the ham on top of Michiko's father's belly. She gave it a pat, then straightened up. "There's Larry!" she exclaimed. She tugged at Michiko's arm and Michiko looked to where the woman was pointing, down the aisle, but only saw a sharp-elbowed teenager scratching his nose and a tattooed woman lifting a box of something from a shelf.

"There's Larry! There's my Larry canary!" The woman began pushing her cart down the aisle. Michiko pushed her father in his cart, leaning into it with all her weight. She followed the woman; she didn't know why. At the end of the aisle they turned the corner and there was a giant clad in shorts, standing in front of a pyramid of fruit, with hair all over his face and legs and arms. He tossed an orange up and down, as if it were a baseball.

"Isn't he a hunk?" the woman exclaimed. "Isn't he a dreamboat? Larry!" There was such joy in the giant's face that Michiko had to look away, and when she did she saw her father lift the package of meat and hold it between his slim hands. "Ham!" he exclaimed. "Now I can find Margaret. I'll surely find Margaret now that I have pineapple and ham. Watanabe is waiting for you. Go back to Japan."

"He's not waiting."

"Believe me, he is," Michiko's father said. "The dead know things like that."

"Larry, she's from Japan!" the woman was saying. "How about that?" Michiko looked at the two of them, with their arms entwined, and for a moment she thought it might be possible to go on without her father, to go forward, to wheel her cart around the store, and put things in it, and later cook them, and, much later, write to Watanabe in Japan. She remembered how he had waved at her when they parted, how, before walking away, she saw a spot of banana cream pie on his shirt that made her smile. "Goodbye, dear child," her father said, but so faintly that Michiko wasn't sure he had even spoken. When she looked, he had vanished from the cart.

The Braid

Mr. Kuroda was standing on a downtown street corner wondering which buildings would topple in an earthquake when a girl in a brightly colored ragtag skirt walked by. She had bead bracelets that looked handmade around her slender wrists but it was the glossy dark braid over one shoulder that made his heart lurch. The braid, a rope to his daughter, pulled him down the street. It bobbed saucily on her back. Mr. Kuroda's daughter had refused to cut it, though her mother had said it was time. "Don't you want to get a more fashionable haircut?" she said and Hana curtly replied no. The braid had gotten her expelled from school, falsely accused of dying her hair a color that wasn't supposed to grow on a Japanese person's head.

"I hate this country," Hana said, though she knew no other and never would. "What am I supposed to do, dye my hair black?" Her parents remonstrated with the school bureaucrats until they said they believed the truth was being told and Hana, dark brown braid and all, could return to class. "I won't go," Hana said.

Her braid now swung down a Portland, Oregon street. It moved fast, and Mr. Kuroda, still jet lagged after the plane ride from Japan, had to trot to keep up. At a busy main street the braid ran into a crosswalk against the light. Mr. Kuroda shouted. Cars honked. But the braid bounced all the way on its wearer's back and made it safely to the other side. When the light turned red and the cars stopped Mr. Kuroda hurried across the street in pursuit.

"Why did you do that?" he called out. "You need to value your life," but the braid didn't seem to hear. It veered left and entered a building with big windows and a door that closed. Mr. Kuroda followed the braid inside to a vast space framed by bookshelves on all sides and past a desk manned by blasé-looking clerks. The braid skipped up a flight of stairs to an equally vast second floor with shelves and shelves of books. It might be Kinokuniya Bookstore, eight stories high, where Mr. Kuroda had taken Hana, five years old then, with hair so shiny it looked shellacked, cut straight all around the bottom and the front. Too short to be braided. She didn't know about braids before her father took her to the bookstore, but she did after she came out. "I wish you'd never read her *that* book," her mother later said. Forever after, once his daughter's hair grew long enough, she wore it in a braid. The braid was who she was. He had not allowed her that. He and his wife both. They had wanted her to conform. Neither had the slightest brown shadow in their hair.

The braid darted left again and the girl bent her head over the basin of a water fountain and drank. The tip of her braid fell in. Without thinking Mr. Kuroda lunged forward and lifted it to dry land.

The girl wheeled around. Her braid flew as she turned. It bounced, full of life. A ribbon, a red fin, adorned its damp tail. When had she put it on? He hadn't noticed it when she walked by him on the street.

"Did you just pull my hair?" the girl cried out. "Why did you pull my hair?" She looked nothing like his daughter. Nothing at all. She had an upturned nose and a cat's green eyes and clenched fists. Freckles sprayed her nose and cheeks. She looked like Pippi Longstocking come to life except for the color of her braid. Mr. Kuroda wanted to grab it again, to hold onto it with all his might.

In his dreams, his daughter floated face down in the sea, her braid trailing behind her, a mermaid's tail, a horse's mane, no, a snake, a silken snake, a hangman's noose, a beautiful scarf of hair around her neck. For weeks after the tsunami the three strands of her dream braid stayed tightly entwined but then they loosened in the water and her father awoke with no hope. Still that day he continued searching for her in the debris-ravaged ruins where Ishinomaki City once stood. "I am a shade," he said when he came upon three Self-Defense soldiers, lifting a shroud-covered body from the muck.

He felt he was going mad. He called his elder brother, who convinced him to abandon the search. At a hospital in Sendai, an overworked doctor put Mr. Kuroda into a drug-induced sleep. When he awoke the doctor told him wearily that it was useless to drive himself to death and that it would be best if he held the proper ceremonies for his daughter so that her spirit could rest. "You have done your best to find her," elder brother concurred.

"Did you hear me?" The girl clamped her braid protectively against her head with a pale hand. "Why did you pull my hair?"

Mr. Kuroda couldn't reply. He wanted to, but couldn't. It was as if everything was frozen in his throat, as if he had swallowed snow and ice. He stared at Pippi, for it was surely she, the girl who had no mother or father for they had both died, or was it the other way around?

"You shouldn't go around pulling women's hair," Pippi said. "It's not a nice thing to do."

Mr. Kuroda bowed in apology. He bowed low. He backed away from the girl, one hand at his throat, trying to warm it so words would come out. The girl let go of her braid. It looked so much like his daughter's. The cold seeped into his chest.

During her last year of high school, Hana had shot up in height. Mr. Kuroda and his wife were both short and marveled at her size. The other high school girls wore their hair in bobs, or falling past their shoulders. Hana told her mother she had no friends. This made them both worried and sad.

"Stop staring at me," the girl said. "You're freaking me out."

"I'm sorry," Mr. Kuroda finally said from his frozen throat. Frozen words. He tried to warm them up but too late. They'd left his mouth. He added more. "Very sorry." He waited for something hard to soften in the girl's face, around her brow. His daughter used to glare at him like that. She fought against him nearly every day. She grew up and moved to the village where her grandmother lived, where they'd often taken her as a child. Mr. Kuroda could still see her running on the beach, holding a kite string, her braids bouncing on her back with every step. She always got the kite aloft.

"Get away from me," the girl said. "Get away now." She unclenched her fists and hoisted up her rucksack. She opened a door with WOMEN on the front of it and wheeled around. Her braid swung a goodbye wave across her back.

It was as if she'd never been there. An empty space that couldn't be filled. With a shaking hand Mr. Kuroda pressed the silver button on the fountain and watched the water arc through the air. He took a sip and felt its cold splash. "Go away," the girl had said. No. "Get away." Mr. Kuroda looked at the bathroom door, through which she and her braid had gone, through which they wouldn't come back.

He walked unsteadily down the wide aisle and veered into a narrower side aisle where he banged his leg on a chair. A hard, tan chair, sitting by itself. He turned himself around. He sat down. He could feel a lump forming on his thigh. People strolled down the aisle, eyeing the books on the shelves, murmuring "excuse me" when they walked on by. Someone might stop, to tell him that he was in the way, to ask him why he was crying and if he needed help. But nobody did. He had arrived from Japan three days previously. He had settled into his hotel and wandered around Portland, looking for he knew not what.

"You're leaving Japan?" elder brother had asked, a note of disbelief in his voice. "Why are you doing that?"

Mr. Kuroda had left Japan because after he returned from Ishinomaki City without Hana, his wife went to stay at her sister's flat and didn't come back. Mr. Kuroda had left Japan because every night he sat alone in the dark. Electricity was being rationed anyway and he could claim he was being patriotic but he was not. He sat cross-legged on the tatami mat floor, smoking cigarettes, careless of where the ashes dropped. He smoked until his lungs hurt and he lost his breath going up stairs. Every morning he prayed for his daughter and left a bowl of rice at her altar but the ritual seemed meaningless.

Once he called his wife. "When are you coming home? Why are you staying at your sister's so long?" She wouldn't, or couldn't, answer him and that day or maybe it was the next he went to a travel agency and bought a plane ticket to America. He had always wanted to take his daughter to America.

"I don't want to go," Hana had said when he brought the subject up. That was a long time ago, when everyone in Japan, or so it seemed, was studying English conversation, preferably from a native speaker with an

American and not a British or Australian accent, and were planning trips to America to say please and thank you and all the rest.

"I'm not interested in America," Hana said. "I want to go to Sweden. I want to learn Swedish and go to Sweden."

"Why?"

"You know, Papa."

"No I don't."

His daughter ignored this childish retort. "If I learn Swedish, I can talk to people there."

"No Japanese speaks Swedish," Mr. Kuroda said.

"You're being ignorant, Papa." Hana was nine years old then. Maybe ten. It bothered Mr. Kuroda that he couldn't remember his daughter's age when she began stating her own mind.

"There's nowhere in Tokyo to learn Swedish," Mr. Kuroda said.

"You're wrong. They teach Swedish at the Berlitz language school."

"It's a hard language to learn. You don't have time to learn a hard language and keep up with school."

"How do you know? You don't know anything about Swedish."

"I know, I've heard," Mr. Kuroda lied. He was a manager at the Hitachi Powdered Metals Company and a chemical engineer. He had a passable knowledge of German, once the universal language of science, though his English was far better because he often spoke about chemical synthesis and powdered metals with English-speaking engineers. When he was a youngster he memorized the Periodic Table of the Elements and wanted to name his daughter after the thirty-fifth element on the list, but his wife, holding the baby to her breast after birth, protested that the word for gold in Japanese, *kin*, was pronounced the same as the word for "germ." A serious student of flower arranging, her choice of name prevailed, and Hana became a "flower child" as an American business associate of Mr. Kuroda's put it, a flower child who believed in things that weren't there. Mr. Kuroda did not believe in things that weren't there.

"I want to go to Sweden to see where Pippi Longstocking lives," Hana declared.

"She's not real. She's a character in a book."

Mr. Kuroda thought of this conversation now and felt ashamed. Not even his wife knew of his weakness for the film series *Otoko wa tsurai yo*, "It's tough being a man," a film series which came out every year. It featured Tora-san, a happy-go-lucky character from Shitamachi, who traveled around Japan pedaling his wares, fell in love, had his heart broken and got into scrapes. Every year, Mr. Kuroda eagerly awaited the release of the newest Tora-san film. He'd sneak away to see the film and then he'd see it again. He felt pure pleasure when he saw the films, the pleasure he imagined his daughter felt when she read the Pippi Long-stocking books. He had never taken her to Sweden. She was not in Sweden now. He should have gone there in her stead. What was he doing in Portland, Oregon, in this massive bookstore the size of the village in Mie Prefecture where he had been born? Perhaps there was a book about Sweden he could find in the store. Surely he could find a book about Sweden somewhere in this vast store. He could imagine his daughter there, with the two braids she'd begun wearing after reading the Pippi Long-stocking books and that she'd later consolidated into one. If he let his imagination "run wild," an idiom he remembered from his advanced conversation class at the Tokyo YMCA College of English, then he'd imagine himself and his wife there, too, holding their daughter's hand. Yes, he'd find a book about Sweden and he'd start now. He'd search the entire store, even if it took weeks. He'd run wild down the aisles, reading the titles on the spines of thousands of books.

Mr. Kuroda rose from the hard chair. Upright, he stood eye level with the fifth shelf from the floor. He was in the Latin American history section of the bookstore, but the titles fled his mind soon after his eyes roamed over the words. He no longer felt hungry or thirsty or tired. He was going to Sweden, if only in his mind. He was going to Sweden in the far north of the world.

He hurried out into the main aisle, cast a nervous glance at the door marked WOMEN, and eyed the imposing desk at the top of the stairs. Behind it, three forbidding clerks with thickly tattooed forearms stared at computer screens. Each wore a golden sticker on a sleeve that read, in capital letters, NEED HELP?

Mr. Kuroda needed help. He did, indeed, need help. His whole coun-try, he reflected as he approached the clerks, needed help, but there was nothing he could do. He had selfishly searched for his own child and when he realized his wife was gone too he sat in a travel agency looking at a pamphlet showing a crystalline, plunging waterfall in Oregon and decided to go there. He had the idea—it seemed ridiculous now—that he'd stand under this waterfall like a mountain monk of old. Chanting sutras. Praying for his life.

"Can I help you?" one of the clerks asked. Variations of this question had been asked of Mr. Kuroda before. By co-workers. By rescue workers. By neighbors. He tried to answer but didn't know how. He couldn't even answer when the emperor of Japan himself and his wife knelt before him and asked the same question. "I don't know," he might have replied then, and replied now. "I'm looking for books about Sweden."

"Sweden!" The clerk enthusiastically tapped on a keyboard with fingernails painted black. A ring like a fishhook pierced her lower lip. Mr. Kuroda pictured his daughter's body hooked by the lip on something, somewhere, in the sea. A nail sticking out of a pier. An anchor trailing a ship. A jagged piece from a building the tsunami had flung away.

"Anything in particular about Sweden you're looking for?"

"I'm not certain," Mr. Kuroda said.

"Swedish history? Scandinavian myths? Traveling in Sweden? *The Girl with the Dragon Tattoo*?" Each time Mr. Kuroda shook his head the clerk typed faster until her fingers became a blur. "Swedish holidays? Swedish filmmakers? Ingmar Bergman? Yes? No? Swedish meatballs? Sorry, that's a joke. I think I'm getting warm. I think I'm getting closer. This sounds interesting." The clerk stopped typing and stuck her face close to the computer screen. "According to what it says here, this book has stunning photographs of Swedish landscapes in it. It's by a Swedish photographer. I have no idea how to pronounce his name." She scrawled something on a small square of paper. She slid it across the counter with her pointy, black-nailed fingers. The bookstore, Mr. Kuroda surmised, put her behind a barrier to protect customers from her sharp edges.

The clerks in Japanese bookstores were slim and polite. They bowed deferentially, calling Mr. Kuroda "honorable customer." They had elegant handwriting, quite unlike the scrawl on the square paper which Mr. Kuroda could not read.

"Thank you," he said.

"Of course."

"What is this?" Mr. Kuroda asked, pointing to a number on the paper.

"It's the shelf in the bookstore where you'll find the book. It's in the Red Room."

"What I really want to find is *Nagakusushita-no-Pippi*," Mr. Kuroda said, slipping into Japanese.

"Pardon?" The clerk ran her hand over her bristly hair. "I'm sorry. What did you say?"

"Pippi," Mr. Kuroda said. He was suddenly too tired to remember how to say Pippi's last name in English. "The girl with the braid. Strong little girl who could lift up her horse."

"She keeps the horse on her front porch," the clerk said, but Mr. Kuroda hadn't heard.

"I'm wrong," he said. "Two braids, not one. Two braids the color of carrot. My daughter had one braid but it was brown." Suddenly Mr. Kuroda saw that very braid walk by. He saw the girl he had followed up the stairs and she saw him. She stopped and gave him a wary look. He wanted to explain. He wanted to say, "Your braid is so like my daughter's braid but it isn't on the head of my daughter. That's the tragedy I have to face."

He remembered that when he returned to Tokyo after the fruitless search for Hana he lay alone on the Western bed he and his wife shared. She'd taken all of the photographs of Hana with her to her sister's flat. The only hint she'd left him of their child was a framed photo on the dresser that he had snapped himself. In her eighth month of pregnancy, she posed in a ruby-colored kimono at the gate to their house. A smile hovered on her lips. The kimono, part of her trousseau, hung in perfect silk pleats around her legs. Mr. Kuroda took the photo from the dresser and curled up with it in bed. He recalled that weeks before the birth, his wife lay on her side with a pillow clamped between her legs. Hana floated in her mother's womb, behind folds of flaming silk, as she floated now somewhere out in the green sea. Mr. Kuroda would never forget how she looked just after birth, with waving arms and legs and thick brown-black hair that stood up on her head. "Her hair is so thick it looks like fur," he told his exhausted wife. The baby lay lightly in his arms, her eyes tightly shut. Her gentle weight made her father forget how much he'd wanted a boy.

"Sir?" The clerk lightly touched him on the arm. "Sir? Are you talking about Pippi Longstocking? Are you looking for Pippi Longstocking? I love that book!"

The girl with the braid stood nearby watching him. He was never the father to Hana that he should have been.

"Yes," he said to the waiting clerk. "Yes, that's it. I'm looking for Pippi Longstocking but can't find her anywhere."

"Super!" the clerk said, springing to her feet. "I know exactly where to find her. I can help for sure." She came out from behind her desk and walked by Mr. Kuroda to the stairs.

He looked helplessly at the girl with the braid.

"You coming?" the clerk turned to him. "I'll take you right there."

Mr. Kuroda bowed to the girl. In apology or farewell, he didn't know which. A wisp of a smile hovered over her face. She lifted her hand—was it a wave?—and swirled around, sending her ragtag skirt flaring around her legs. She walked away, amongst the books. Her thick brown braid played tag against her back. Mr. Kuroda felt a cauldron of ecstasy and pain, a crashing wave of grief and love. And then he followed the clerk down the stairs.

Acknowledgments

I gratefully acknowledge the support of fellowships from the Iowa Writers' Workshop, the MacDowell Colony, Literary Arts, and the Oregon Arts Commission.

I would like to thank the following persons for inspiration, support and encouragement. My family: William and Thelma Pierce, Diane Pierce, Ellen Pierce, Roy Daley and Chris Ericksen. My teachers: the late Jack Cady, the late James Alan McPherson, Marilynne Robinson, the late Frank Conroy and my yoga teacher, the late B.K.S. Iyengar. My writer friends: James Tata, Katharine Stall, Diane Hinton Perry, Jessica Morrell, Deborah Garfinkle, Lise Goett, Irene Parikhal, Osama Esber, Margie Doolan, Iqbal Pittalwala, Susan Madison and Catherine Lombard. My other artist friends: Bernadette Fox, Janice Pierce, Eduardo Santierre, Jean Clugston, Emily Jane Butler, Ian Underwood, Miguel Estrada, and Pete Perry. I'd also like to thank Yuko Matsumoto, Christina Okubo Perry, Shawn Liu, Desiree Guensch, the Imai family, Junko Bindhany, Matsu Nakamura, Linda Fukuoka, Malini Johar Schueller, and the late Sandy Japel. In memory of Zita Ohe and Janet Lynn Kerr, who both shared adventures with me in Tokyo.

About the Author

Marian Pierce has written for Japan's National Public Radio and traveled solo throughout India by bus and train. Her short stories have appeared in *Portland Monthly* magazine, *Gentlemen's Quarterly (GQ)* magazine, *Creative Writers' Handbook*, *Scribner's Best of the Fiction Workshops 1997*, *STORY*, the *Japan Times*, *The Mississippi Review*, *Confrontation*, *Puerto del Sol*, *Yomimono* and, most recently, *Hospital Drive*. She won the 2009 Wordstock Short Fiction Competition and was the 1995 winner of the Frederick Exley fiction competition, sponsored by *GQ*. She has received fellowships from the Iowa Writers' Workshop, the MacDowell Colony, Literary Arts, the Oregon Arts Commission, KHN Center for the Arts, and was short listed for the David Wong Fellowship at the University of East Anglia for an author writing fiction set in the Far East. She is a freelance editor, ghostwriter and teacher in Portland, Oregon, USA.

www.marianpierce.com